The CURSED INN

A TALE OF CHARLES ISLAND

MARISSA D'ANGELO

Cover design by Thea Magerand.

Photography by Dorie Penn.

This story is fiction. Although the place exists, the characters, plot and dialogues in this book are fictional. Resemblance to any persons living or dead is coincidental.

Printed in the United States of America.

Dedication

This book is dedicated to my
Grandma "Neenee" Jeanne

You helped me up until the very end whether it be
listening to my endless ideas for my books or helping
me get out of my writer's blocks.
I miss you more than you'll ever know; let your
spirit continue on.

Books by Marissa D'Angelo

Tales of Charles Island Series

The Cursed Spirit

The Cursed Spirit 2

The Cursed Vessel

The Cursed Inn

The Cursed Monastery

Presence

Other Books

The Vanished

Chasing Time

Author's Note

Since the release of this book, I have wanted to find some way to help Charles Island and the wildlife that it supports. A local reforestation group is working hand in hand with the Connecticut Department of Energy and Environmental Protection to plant more trees so that the island and its wildlife can survive and thrive.

Message from Reforestation Group:

We want to restore the island to its former state. After years of invasive species and diseases, we need to help nature along with this task.

<u>10% of the proceeds from this series will go to this cause.</u>

Remnants

1

Moisture filled the air with an unnerving taste of confusion and desperation for what once was. Every lone droplet of rain gathered on earth's impenetrable surface, softening its grounds. The consistency of each drop altered shortly after they absorbed into one another. This ongoing charade reminded me much of humanity as we would all eventually become something bigger than just ourselves...or that was the hope, anyway. A horrifying image of the ruined remains of what used to be my life laid before me. As the rain showered down on me, I squeezed my eyes and clenched my jaws — hoping that when I reopened them, I could awaken from the nightmare that my life had become. It is said that rainwater has a purifying property and will cleanse all. The woes and broken promises of yesterday were forgotten, or at least pushed to the back of my mind as I struggled to grasp reality. I felt my hair becoming more and more soaked as I stood there, unable to move — barely able to stand completely on my own. My long, brunette strands clashed against the white of my dress. It had taken me hours and hours to prepare for the perfect day that would come to its crashing demise.

As a young girl, I would hear the church bells sing in celebration of two people coming together. Whenever those chimes would sound, I'd rush to the window on impulse and look out, waiting for the horse and carriage to stampede down the roadway. From the house that I grew up in, we were just close enough to see the outside of the church. A woman would appear from its colossal doors beside the man that had courted her. Her white dress puffed out under her torso with layer upon layer concealed by a sheet of white lace. Its sleeves fit like a glove, reaching down to her wrists in a frilly design that I made a mental note I would never have if the day were to ever come for me. White lacing to match the entirety of the pure dress tied in a bow on her back, it looked almost painful to wear. Her veil swooped back and trailed behind her, laying delicately over the back of her dress and blending with the lace. At the start of her veil were various flowers. Her neck was adorned in pearls that clashed eloquently with the darkness of her hair, which had been pulled back in several braids intertwined into one another. But more important than any fancy dress was the fact that it was a day that she and her man would come together as one. Oftentimes, I would see couples that didn't seem to have much interest in each other. One time, there was a man that stood beside his bride and I would see him staring off at other women that very day! But...on rare occasion, you would see a man and a woman that couldn't tear their eyes off one another. There would be a twinkle in his eyes, as any onlooker could tell he thought the absolute world of the woman he was with. That right there was the kind of love I wanted to find...

I shook my head as to snap out of the flashback for this day should have been the one I had been waiting for my entire life, possibly being an inspiration for another girl like I had been all those years ago. It had the most perfect start, but all storms come after a brief calm.

After the emergency bells sounded, the first thought that came to my mind was to find the man I was destined to marry and make sure that he was okay. The rush of the waves matched my initial attempts at finding him. Corridors lay before me, destroyed and in an irreversible state of ruin. The doors and any remaining exits were inaccessible as fallen pieces of roof had blocked any and all openings. When I woke up that morning, I would have never been able to guess that the day would have turned out this way. I knew all too well what would happen after they repeatedly warned me. When the others weren't spelling it out, there were other signs as clear as day. The stubborn nature of my being ran deep within me and there was no way to refuse its temptations. At first, the warnings came to me in dreams and I was quick to shrug them off as just pointless worries. As commoners reported the strange occurrences throughout their visits, there was always some type of excuse to explain their confusions. But no, now it was too late to go back and listen to that very first sign that could have helped to avoid all the damage that lay before me and scorched my mind by replaying the devastating memories again and again.

At first glance, the land before us stood full of promise and anticipation. No more worries of the past and a new life to build from the ground up. It had been years since my father and I were on our own, but we made do. When our ancestors came to America, they had been promised the streets would be paved in gold…it forced my mind to wander and form unrealistic expectations of the new place that we would soon call home. When you have lived in a certain place your entire life and unexpectedly make the journey elsewhere to start anew, it is both frightening and exhilarating at the same time. The horrors of the unknown lurk in the depths of your mind, but they are quickly suppressed by pure imagination of the incredible what-ifs to come.

Forget all of that, though. None of that matters now…or at least anymore. I struggled to keep my back straight as I looked before me. The heat radiated from within the center of the land. Violent patterns of red and orange billowed in the wind as it spread like a contagious disease, extending throughout the entirety of the island. Relentless waves of smoke stormed out from what once were windows that people would sit by to enjoy the outside air. Flames danced in the wind as it blew them left and right, causing them to spread like a sudden, dismantling toxin. As it flickered in each direction, it seemed to mock us — dancing in the constant gusts. A deep pit in my gut felt as if it would consume the entirety of my being. I longed to run as fast as I could from what I once thought to be my home. The surrounding waves echoed, reminding me of my own inability to escape the land's demise. But what poisoned me even more than my imprisonment was my longing to go back to when it all began. The simple journey that had just begun all those years ago. An ordinary life didn't seem so bad after all compared to the fate that now wrapped around me like permanent chains, weighing me down.

Trees that had once towered over me like tall buildings were torn apart by flames, which sent them tumbling down. Seagulls that soared high in the sky yesterday, abandoned their homes and were nowhere to be found. The absence of life caused the land to become eerie and uninviting. Powerful waves clashed against the outskirts of the coast, adding to the repetitive rumble of trees as they demolished a building in the center with their weight. They pressed it down firmly until it no longer looked as though it was a building, but instead a war zone. Water began trickling down from the sky as if those above cried out for the unfortunate souls below. Even this could not delay its demise; for a curse seemed to linger on this land.

Invisible shackles held me there, forbidding my escape both in mind and body. There was nothing to do except hold on to the meager amount of humanity that still remained within.

A New Beginning

2

"Come Ange, the coach awaits! I'm going to bring my briefcase out, but when I'm back in you better be ready!" Father called out to me from the other side of the door.

"Okay, be right out in a bit!" I called as I jumped out of bed, nearly tumbling over a pair of shoes that I placed beside it. After several years of saving up and spending only a meager bit of coin on food, we had finally managed to find the opportunity of a lifetime. Previously, Father had a small shop that he opened up from within our home where he would sell handcrafted buttons and canes. After he found me designing the things that he'd make for my own amusement, he decided to include me in his work so that more upscale people would take an interest in it. When my grandparents died, they had left a small portion of their fortune to Father with the other half going to his brother, who lived a distance away. Father had been saving it, wanting to make sure that he spent it on something worthwhile. After seeing various for sale signs of a colossal house on a nearby island, it had piqued our interest...especially Father's, for what he could turn it into. He had clearly grown tired of button and cane-making and was looking for a change, as was I. He wrote a letter of interest at once that displayed his intentions of purchasing the land, which included the house.

I was thankful for Father to include me in all of his voyages as it was not custom for a lady to be present during business transactions. Father treated me as an equal. There was one area in which his mind aligned with the others, and I was sure he would bring it up along the way.

Little did he know I had just crawled out of bed. When you want to move quickly and are in a rush, anything and everything goes against you. I stumbled out of bed, grabbing onto the nightstand for stability and moved over to the dark mahogany vanity, outlined in delicate swirls carefully carved into the polished wood. I sank down into the cushion as I fumbled through each drawer, deciding on which jewelry to wear.

I pulled a long drawer out of the vanity's base. Within, a journal rested on the right-hand side. On the left was a small jar of ink with a few feathers that lay next to it. Part of me wanted to tell Father he could go on without me so that I could get some writing done, but I knew that would let him down. It didn't stop me from brushing my fingertips against the height of the feather.

Atop the base of the vanity were several smaller drawers on either side of the mirror. The drawers to the right contained facial brushes, blush powders and combs. A brush that I washed and dried the last time I went into town was the perfect size to push into the small jar of powder. Tapping it a few times on the side of the jar caused any excess to fall back in. As soon as I finished applying it to my face, I noticed how much color was instantly taken out of my skin. I tapped the brush into another jar that stood adjacent to the one I had just used. This contained a peachy blush that would give me some more color. I didn't stop at my cheeks, but instead guided the brush gently over my forehead and down past my temples.

I was taking far too long and knew I had to hurry or Father would surely go without me as I knew he was already anxious enough about finally going to look at the land. I needed to make a good impression though, so I continued my routine. In any case, Father could talk...he would lose track of time quite easily when he started talking to others, and I was sure that he was speaking with the coachman. I walked over to the window and peered out from behind the curtain, trying not to get caught. Father stood next to the horse and its coachman, just as I had suspected. His hands were moving up and down, which he commonly did as he spoke and occasionally, he would tilt his head back slightly as he laughed at whatever they were talking about.

I had time, but not that much... As I scurried back to the vanity, I looked over at the drawers to the left that held various types of jewelry. The top drawer contained opal earrings to match the pendant that lay beside it. Shimmering sparkles with scores of colors cast a reflection from the window's light. In the drawer below that, was an amethyst pendant in the shape of a crystal. It hung down from a slim gold chain and contrasted the lighter opal with its purple tone. I did not have matching earrings to this one, but had found plain gold ones that could match with anything. As I slid both drawers open, I pondered which one I would possibly wear. I pushed them back in and opened the undermost drawer. It held the most precious jewelry that I owned. A necklace of intertwining golden braids that met at a Victorian emerald lay unused. It was on rare occasion that I ever wore that one, but that drawer was the most frequently used. I would often pull it open and rub my fingertips along it, closing my eyes to imagine how it would have looked on my mother. Far back behind that necklace was the one photograph that I had of her. She stood tall with a dark dress and her hair was up high in an interwoven bun. When I was very young, she had taught me how to do this with my own hair. I would form a long braid, then bring it up and wrap it around itself repeatedly in a circle, tucking the end in the back.

I was alerted by a sudden set of footsteps as they stomped from down the hall. I tried to form the bun in the back of my hair, but kept failing with shaken and clammy fingers. I might as well have had oil spread over the entirety of my palms. I grabbed a ribbon and tied half my hair back in a bow. Closing the most treasured drawer, I opened the one that held the opal pendant and placed it around my neckline, clasping the back. I had nearly forgotten to gather the matching earrings, but quickly placed them on each lobe. There was one outfit that was set out the night before. I shimmied into the maroon silk taffeta skirt and cranberry brocade bodice that fit slim to my figure. Over the bodice, I eased myself into a jacket that went down to my waist and matched the maroon skirt. It was adorned in white spiral designs from the cuffs extending up both sleeves.

Persistent knocking practically made me jump out of the skirt I had just put on. I had used up all of Father's patience. He would surely be in any second. I ran over to quickly put my heels on, then back to the chair by the vanity, to make believe I was just sitting down waiting for him the whole time. Fully dressed, I worked up quite a sweat in my haste to get back to the chair.

"What's taking so…" The door opened and Father peeked his head in, but couldn't finish his sentence as he saw I was all ready. He had his plaid cap on, hiding the grays of his hair although a few still poked out the sides. But I dare not tell him. Continuing to let him think he pulled it off made him happiest. His face was rounded and clean shaven, with sideburns going down far too low for the average man. Furry eyebrows with mixed shades of black and gray seemed to match his deep gray eyes — the ones that I had inherited from him. I always felt that it scared people to look them right in the eyes, as mine often reminded me of cold stones. Father had dimples in his cheeks and usually wore a smile on his face that clashed against his cold eyes. It made him much more inviting to anyone — even a stranger. And the laughter that would bellow out of him at times was surely contagious.

"Well, why didn't you say so?!" he exclaimed, walking in fully. "The coach has been here. Let's go!"

Opportunity

3

"America's roads of gold" was surely an overstatement given how many bumps shook me repeatedly. I was glad that I went with my gut and didn't opt to bring my journal as I would've ended up with an abstract painting of some sort made with ink. At times, Father would try to talk and every other word or so would be juggled by another bump the coach hit. That didn't stop him, though.

"It will take us close to an hour, maybe a little more, to get there. When we do, it will take a bit longer to get across the path." He peered down at my feet and looked back up at me. "Heels…oh what are we going to do with you?" I had followed his gaze and looked down at my feet, already aching from the meager amount of walking I had done. Wasn't I supposed to wear these fancy things? I put out both my arms in silence, as if to ask what he wanted from me. My silent response said it all as he began to go off on a tangent; talking himself into another topic, which I had no choice but to follow him into.

"We'll figure it out, but anyway, I think this is the best opportunity that could have fallen right into our hands." He smiled and looked out the window as if his mind were elsewhere and not completely focused on what we were talking about.

"Would we be moving to this place, too?" I asked, thinking of how heavy the vanity would be to move. But it had to come with me. I didn't have many clothes or other items, but that was a must. After attending school for a short time and moving on to helping Father with his small shop, there wasn't much need having an extravagant wardrobe. My introverted ways caused me to find myself by the window or vanity, writing away. There would be times I'd stay in my room for so long that Father would run up to make sure I was okay as he hadn't heard the slightest sound of life coming from where I stayed. When Father's business brought in more customers due to the designs that I'd paint onto the various items he made, I was forced to come out of my shell...but only slightly. He became so busy with completing orders that I took to the front desk and helped customers if they had special requests. By nightfall, I still managed to find myself by the window, peering out at everyone on their night adventures, whether they be bachelors looking for a woman to court, drunken men, or visitors prowling about. It is commonly said that you can learn much more about the world and humanity by just simply watching. I snapped out of it and realized Father was talking away a mile a minute about this new place that we were seemingly moving to.

"Ange, you there? Wake up! Let me tell you my plan, you ready?" I nodded in agreement and he continued, "I am going to purchase the building on the island..." he paused for a moment and looked back at me after briefly glancing out the window. "We are," he corrected himself.

"It used to be a plantation of which the island is named after, but we are going to turn it into an inn where people can stay. We can think of some other activities they could do while they are on the island, too. This area is set to thrive and in the next several years, business will boom so much that we can just hire a bunch of people to work for us and carry on the inn. What do you think, Ange?" Well, one thing was for sure and that was that father was a dreamer. Once he became fixated on an idea, he just had to do it. So, I knew no matter what I said at that point, he was going to find a way to make it happen, anyway. I was glad that this conversation didn't turn a different way, which is what usually happened. Oh, but there was still time…

"I think it's a great idea! I remember those days we struggled to keep your shop afloat and how we often wondered how we would afford to keep our own roof over our heads. Now, we're going to possibly have our own inn! We've made it, Father. We have come such a long way." I knew he'd love to hear this, especially coming from me. The trying past could not go ignored, as it was what we had to endure in order to end up where we were today. However, there were still worries that I had, but didn't want to ruin his moment by mentioning them.

"Do you think we can run an entire inn, though? I wouldn't know the first thing about that," I admitted. I could tell that he already knew I would say this in response, as his answer was quick.

"Of course, you can take care of things in the household and organize everything while I talk with others and make sure that no one overstays their welcome." He looked down again at my heels, then back up at me, pressing his hand down on my shoulder firmly as he would when he was telling me something serious. That meant he was bound to use my full name, too… The thing about being with someone so often was that you could predict what they would do without fail.

"Angeline, I know it has been hard without Mother here. And I know I haven't done everything perfectly — but I've tried my best and I think you are right. We have come a long way, but I couldn't have done all of this without you. You've got your mother's light inside of you. It's contagious and truly does spread to others. But one thing, we need to find you a suitor!" Oh goodness...there he goes! A tear that formed at the corner of my eye sped down my cheek and met the corner of my mouth as I started laughing. A ridiculous idea at that. I saw how marriages commonly ended with grief and misery. I was perfectly fine with my journal and ink.

"Come on, aren't we doing just fine now? I don't need an arranged marriage like the others. I'll do just fine by myself, thank you." He and I both knew it wasn't the common way, though. I guess it would be nice to have someone... but it was difficult too because from the moment I started to help Father with his shop, I had it etched into my brain that it was not okay to trust people. Time after time, people would promise to pay him only to never show their faces again. One significant time that I remember was when he tried to hire someone for extra help and we found him stealing some money out of the drawer. Since then, it was just Father and I working the shop. How was I going to find a suitor when I couldn't trust anyone except for my own Father?

I looked out the window of the coach that was gently covered by a curtain made entirely of yellow lace. The trees were less and less abundant as a thick, salty odor filled the air. The unforgettable stench reminded me of the few times that Father brought me to the coastline that gave me awful sunburns along my entire body. It turned my stomach, thinking back to the terrible sun poisoning that I had as I was unable to get out of bed for days thereafter. A loud whinny and gasp came from the horse ahead of our coach as we came to a stop.

"Don't worry, I didn't forget what you said. We'll talk more about suitors later," Father said — ensuring that I knew he wouldn't give up. In a few moments, the coachman opened up the doors and held his hand out to help us off. Father, having the pride that he did, ignored the coachman's hand and managed to get off on his own. I, on the other hand, did not mind the help and carefully placed my hand in his, smiling at him in thanks as I followed after Father. The coachman tipped his head forward as if he would've bowed at me if he weren't busy helping as I wobbled out in my poor choice of shoes. Is this the kind of suitor Father wanted me with? I was surprised that he didn't try to introduce us. Although, he could've been old enough to be my grandfather... so maybe not. I chuckled at this thought and noticed just how loud I was as both Father and the coachman looked over at me and sighed. They must have been thinking 'Silly women, what goes on in their minds anyway…?' Well, I ask the same about men. As I walked out, Father turned back to tip the coachman then walked before me so he could lead the way. I didn't know where we were going, so I was glad he took charge. Although, he might not have known either.

"We are going to meet the man around here," he said as he called back to me, but continued walking. "I just want to show you something." We walked for about ten minutes or so and then came before two large bushes. There was a bit of a clearing in between each, as if it was a path to something on the other side. He set down that path and the curiosity in me was piqued as I wondered what was on the other side. A few prickers almost caught my leg, but I was able to avoid them by stomping down with my heel. When we got to the other side of the bushes, there was mainly sand and an entire beach laid out before us. He took a few more steps forward as did I and then stopped, gazing out at the water. Aside from the dense fog and salty aroma that filled the air, there was one thing that I just couldn't miss. It looked small from where I stood, but an island stretched out before us. Seagulls flapped their wings neurotically and headed straight for it, away from the sandy shores where we were. That must have been their home. It looked as though there was an entire forest on the island. I hadn't noticed, but my jaw had dropped and I finally closed it when I saw Father chuckling at me.

"This is ours?" I asked.

"It can be," he answered.

Don't Turn Back

4

The tide was coming in as waves pushed past several sea shells, leaving a thick path of seaweed along the shore. Father and I kept to the other side of the green line that traced against the coast, his pace much quicker than mine. My heels dug into the sand and I had to force each step up in order to go anywhere. Aside from the consistent crashing of waves, was the sound of several seagulls flocking about. Looking up, they seemed to be circling us like vultures. One by one, they dove toward the sand and picked at something that ended up causing a fight between the entire flock, as it looked like they would fight to the death for whatever it was. A trail of what appeared to be bread led up to my father, who continued walking before me. I kept my eyes locked on him and noticed the pieces of bread that he tore off, throwing each one behind him for the birds. As I continued to watch, I realized the pattern. He tore off a bit of the bread and put it into his mouth, then the next piece would go to the birds. He would continue to do this with the entire baguette.

"Want some?" he hollered without glancing back. I felt my stomach rumble, but didn't want to make a mess of myself — especially not before making this business transaction.

"No, thank you. I'll make some lunch after this," I shouted ahead, trying to project my voice over the seagulls' squawks. Luckily, he threw each tidbit of bread to the right or left instead of directly in the path that I was following. The repetitive rush and nonstop screams from the birds sent my heart racing and, for a moment, I felt tempted to turn back. I needed to remain here and support my father, though. As we continued on, I felt as though I was being watched. With great reluctance, I peered back at the two bushes that we had originally come through and saw a man that looked much different from anyone I had met at school or in town. His skin was much darker, almost matching the tanned shade of tea that I would usually drink each morning. Unlike the button-downed shirts that men commonly wore and slacks, it looked as though he made his entire ensemble from scratch. Light brown slacks that had frills on either side and a strap hung over his back. It appeared as though he had just been hunting. Handcrafted arrows protruded out of the bag that he carried, each one dyed a different shade of autumn. Long, black hair which came close to the length of mine, reached down below his chest. His face was gentle in that both his dark eyebrows furrowed up in deep worry. His stocky, broad shoulders were hunched as if he was going to make a run for it. He looked more afraid of me than I of him, as he closely resembled a deer when it froze after being spotted by humans. I felt my heart stop as he stared directly at me, seemingly into my soul. In the next moment, a fawn came out from behind him. It was alarming that it crept up so close by to him, clearly not afraid. The man shook his head as if to signal the fawn to come back, and it followed his silent directions. Before turning back, he shook his head at me and pointed behind me. When I followed his gesture to see that he was pointing to the island, I quickly turned back, and he was gone. *Why did he shake his head when pointing to the island? Was I not to go there?*

"Look over there, Ange. You see them?!" Father said, this time looking back at me and realizing he was much further ahead than he had previously thought. Father didn't seem to see the man or fawn that had just given me a warning. I followed the direction Father was looking toward and saw the paddle boat that carried two men within as they approached the shore, slowing down tremendously. Father began to bear right, changing his path into the seaweed and continuing on to meet the boaters. My route was similar to his, but I avoided the seaweed, carefully stepping over its slimy bits. Before me, Father had already made it up to the boat and stood ankle-deep in the water as he helped them drag their boat more onto the shore so that it didn't get carried away by the tides. Both men differed in a striking way. From where I stood, I couldn't make out too many features, but immediately noticed the height difference. One was much taller than Father, towering over him by several inches while the other was a bit shorter than him and looked slouched over, walking much more slowly.

The taller one seemed to have watched me as I struggled over the seaweed in my heels. He ran over to my side, extending his hand out to offer help. In my attempt to offer respect and curtsy, I nearly stumbled over and fell into the wet sand, but luckily, he caught my fall.

"Thank you, sir…" He didn't have a name, but oh I could give him one. He looked like all the other men that would pass me by in town. It's not that he wasn't good looking — because he definitely was, but just didn't seem any different from the others. His dirty blonde hair was neatly combed back, leaving a part three-fourths of the way over on his hairline. The oval shape of his face was clean-shaven and sideburns cut short to match this clean look. Although he had just been in a boat, paddling, he wore dress pants and a white button-down shirt, holding his suit jacket over one arm. His stature was towering, but incredibly slim — almost to the point I questioned if he had any muscle at all underneath. I realized I had been wrapped up in my thoughts while he tried introducing himself.

"It's a pleasure to meet you, Lady Angeline." He held out his hand again, extending a welcome. "My name is George. You and your father will be purchasing the building on the island from my father and I." I reluctantly took his hand in mine and shook it, regretting it soon after my palm became sweaty from his grasp. Pulling my hand back, I tried to be respectful for the sake of business.

"It's nice to meet you too, George." Short and sweet. He looked down at my heels and then back up at me, smiling.

"Didn't plan for this, huh?" he asked. What was I to do? I needed to impress the others, but was just about to break my ankles in the process of that. He didn't wait for my response. "Don't worry, we can take the boat over there. Come on."

From there, I did end up placing my hand in his as it would've been better than stumbling all over the place due to these wretched heels that I planned to burn as soon as I got back. As we got closer to the others, I picked up my skirt, careful not to soak it from the rising water. Both of our fathers were in the middle of a conversation when they both stopped and looked over at us.

"This is my daughter, Angeline. I had to bring her with me; she is my business partner. No deal without her!" He gestured over to me and George's father nodded. He was nowhere as tall as George and was a bit hunched over, looking very frail, as if the wind alone could knock him over. We shook hands, but unlike with

George — I was extra careful with the old man's fragile hand, afraid that I would break it.

"It's nice to meet you. What are we waiting for?! Let's go to the island, come on," he shouted, more excited than I could've ever pretended to be. Just past the island's perimeter, a bit of a rocky path formed that could connect it with the mainland. Looking over at the paddle boat, I definitely opted for that — there was no way I would make it over there in my heels alone.

Welcome Home

5

The repetitive squawks of seagulls trailed behind and eventually were drowned out by the waves as we made our way to the island. There were several trees here and there, but it looked as though many were cleared out in order to make way for the house in the center. With low tide, the house appeared even larger as the land around it cleared and rocky paths trailed around where the sea met the land. Several other boats, mirroring the size of the one that we were in, were docked against the shore. They were secured tightly with ropes around the pilings. The house looked as though it was modeled after a square, as it had two floors and several windows surrounding them. The top floor had a balcony that went around the entire house, as the bottom floor had a porch surrounding it. Columns extended from the roof down every several feet to provide support for its structure. The house, along with the various columns, were painted white, which caused it to stand out all the more against the greenery of the island. I was able to easily single out the entrance as it had an archway just before it entangled in a plethora of vines. Going down the center of the archway was a path that continued down the middle of the land and directly towards the rocky path that led up to the island if walking there from the mainland. Along the path to the house were tall trees on either side, making it appear as though you were walking into a house that belonged to royalty. There were two chimneys that protruded out of either side of the roof, confirming there were two kitchens within the house, or at least an extra fireplace. I instantly wished that I could write about what I saw before me. As the men were deep in discussion about their coming transaction, I couldn't help but peer back at the mainland, wondering if the man that warned me was still there. It was completely empty. I still couldn't seem to figure out why he had shaken his head when looking at the island. It was as if he didn't want me to go there. He could have tried a little harder to stop me from venturing out there. Surely, Father couldn't be talked out of this since he had been anticipating it for a while.

"What're you looking at back there?" A voice came. "The true journey is what lies ahead!" he continued. I turned back and realized that while both of our fathers were still immersed in their conversation, George had managed to scoot closer to me without me noticing. He continued rowing towards the island, but kept looking over my way. His light blue eyes twinkled in the sunlight as he squinted, struggling to keep them open despite the blinding rays. His light skin matched the light tones of his eyes and hair along with the outfit he chose. He differed greatly from the man that I had seen back on the mainland. I still couldn't seem to shake him from my mind. I had a deep curiosity to know more about the mysterious man that hadn't even given me his name. I looked back up at George, who was awaiting my response.

"Oh nothing, just a little sea sick…" I didn't feel sick in the slightest, but it was the only excuse I could think of that would make sense, or so I thought.

"It's been just a few minutes since we got in!" George exclaimed, causing me to realize that my excuse actually did not make much sense after all. It would have to do… I shrugged my shoulders and turned towards the island again. As we drew closer, the house appeared even larger than before. I wondered what life was like for George, having had this house as a bit of a "vacation home" in his family for a while. It must have been quite nice, but they were selling it. That's what didn't make an ounce of sense. If it was so nice out here, why would they sell it, anyway? Good things always seemed to come with a catch. I looked over at Father and he was now holding onto his plaid cap so the wind didn't blow it away. As George drew closer to the shores, he yanked his shoes off and set them beside me. As soon as I caught a whiff of their disgusting smell, he must have noticed by the frown on my face as he chuckled. It was tempting to reach over and move them away from me, but that would mean I had to contaminate my hands with the shoes that he sweat in. I decided to slide over towards the opposite side of the boat. George got out and was knee-deep in water as I felt the bottom of the boat slide up against the one bit of sandy shore that the island had to offer. Most of it had been outlined with rocks, very much like the pathway that led there. He first held out a hand to his father and looked as though he picked up the entire weight of his body, leading him onto land. After that, my father managed a way out of the boat himself —

very typical of him. I would have done the same if not for the heels. Heels. I looked down at my feet and made another mental note to burn them upon my return. What an awful idea. I reluctantly decided to peel each off and set them beside his shoes. When I looked up, George was still there and his expression matched my own disgusted face from earlier when he had taken his shoes off. He was mocking me and trying to be playful. I gave a smile, then wobbled off the boat, briefly taking his hand to balance. As soon as I was able to release my hand from his, I did and continued on towards the house. The others were already making their way down the main path to the house that lay between several towering trees. I turned back to George, and he was tying up the boat to a piling.

"Why are you selling this? It seems awfully nice," I noted. If I was going to linger behind with George, I might as well find out some information.

"It has belonged to us for a long time and we just want something different. Your father mentioned an idea that was rather tempting, so we chose him first from the long list of people who inquired about the property," he answered without hesitation. Long list of people…

"Which was?" I asked, already knowing the answer but wondering if Father relayed this information to them as well.

"A resort open to all. The island was too big for us to keep it to ourselves and it would be better off in someone else's hands. I will be doing other things on the mainland working in the banks, so I chose to sell the property and invest it," he replied, wiping the sweat off his forehead. Well, it was good to at least know what he planned on doing with the money. I bet it hurt his father to see a place that had been with the family easily transferred to someone else without much hesitation. It was a typical banker move...they couldn't think about feelings; instead, they needed to think of financials if they were going to make more.

I paused for a moment in hesitation whether or not I should continue going, but looked ahead to find Father several yards in front of us already and that gave me my answer. Walking down the path between the trees, the island was so vibrant and full of life. Summer had just come upon us, and each day was a struggle to stay out of the scorching sun. It was much different on the island, though. There was a breeze that surrounded and just when the heat felt like too much, it would put you at ease. The melody of chirping birds in the trees seemed to welcome us with open arms to the extravagant house. When we finally came up to the archway that was wrapped in the greenest of vines, George went up a few steps and opened the aquamarine doors. As I crept up after him, the doors seemed to open up a portal into another world of which I had never known. A world of riches and glamor lay before me as brightly polished wooden floors sparkled in the sun's reflection through the windows and doorway. Taking a few steps further, a grand spiral staircase came down several feet in, connecting both floors. The entirety of the railing was the purest of whites to match the outside of the house and all the interior walls. To the left, there was another room that looked as if it was a small office and to the right, another that matched in comparison. Everything beyond the foyer was concealed by another door just past the staircase. A colossal paraffin oil lamp hung down from the formidable ceiling and contained various crystals all strung together as they wove around the light that it would contain.

I peeked over at Father and by the awe-struck expression on his face, including the fact that he removed his cap and held it to his chest, I knew we would be sealing the deal. We both looked over at George and his father, that were still standing in the doorway. George's father's eyes were dull and barren, his mind readable as it looked like he had to restrain himself with everything in his power to not shoo us out and keep the island for himself. Meanwhile, George held out the keys to Father and looked back and forth

at us as he confirmed the obvious.

"Welcome home," he smiled.

6

In the days that passed, we had moved our things to the estate on Charles Island. When the previous owners left, Father asked if they would come join us for dinner at the inn after we were all settled in. The day had come far too soon, but I was able to explore the house just a bit. Moving items back and forth, I hadn't slept at the house on the island yet. Tonight after dinner would be the very first night and I was looking forward to it, but part of me wanted to go back inland to where we had stayed all along. The sudden change brought about a plethora of emotions; both good and bad. When Father occupied himself at the front reception desk to place the items that had been in his workshop, I spent my time wandering around. There were some things that he just couldn't give up, such as his cane and button-making. George and his family left all the furniture in the house and we were luckily able to keep almost everything the same as it was due to the incredible donation.

The ground floor was my first obstacle to explore. As there were offices on either side of the foyer, beyond that were other rooms that I was just as curious to see. I chose to head right first and passed the reception desk room with comfort, knowing there were likely more exciting things to find within the other rooms.

The room adjacent to the office on the right did not have any doors closing it off. Instead, its extensive doorway opened up to a dining area. The walls were the first to draw my attention. A blood red wallpaper surrounded me as I entered. A dark chestnut wooden table extended almost the entire length of the room. Light trickled in from the lengthy windows that were slightly covered in a transparent, lacy sheer. Long, golden curtains extended from the spiraling rod at the tops of each window. The thickness of their fabric was parted in the centers so as to let more light in.

I continued walking, careful not to break anything, as it looked as though no soul had ever really lived here. From the white tablecloth to the perfectly set table full of glassware and napkins folded to perfection, it was all for show. We would be eating in this room later and part of me wondered when the last time was that someone did so. As if I was walking on eggshells, I tiptoed to the next room to find the kitchen beyond a simple chestnut brown door that matched the table in the dining area. The kitchen reminded me much of back home, as it was quite ordinary in that it did not have anything that was completely remarkable. It contained a gas stove, countertop space with a wooden board for cutting, and several knives and cutlery were spread out on the counter — fresh for their next use. A dark kettle sat atop the stove and on the opposite side of the room was a long wooden dresser that had four cabinets, likely containing dishes and other dining ware. A few pots and pans hung down from hooks on the ceiling. I chuckled to myself, thinking of the ruckus I would make if I attempted to cook here. With so many items in perfect placement, I was bound to knock things down and send everyone running to check if I was still alive. There was a nice bowl full of fruit on a small table next to the gas stove. I grasped my hand on the doorknob to enter the next room and was surprised when it wouldn't open. I took a step back and debated continuing through, but quickly gave into my curiosity as I turned the knob and pushed again. It didn't give. On the third try, I pushed my whole body into it and still couldn't seem to get it open. In the next moment, the entirety of my being felt as though it jumped out of my skin.

"And where are you headed?" A familiar, male voice asked. I immediately turned around and pressed my back up against the door that I had previously tried barreling through.

"I could ask you the same," I retorted his question. George smiled and put one arm over my head to lean himself against the door, coming far closer than necessary. I pressed my lips together and looked up at his pale arm.

"I'm exploring the house…who let you in anyway?" I asked. This was his home. Keyword: was. He stayed put and smiled at me as if I was a source of entertainment for him that he had been missing out on.

"We came early to dinner and my father is showing your father the offices and some supplies that we left for you," he answered and took his hand away, giving me more space. I let out a deep sigh of relief that I was sure he acknowledged.

"Well, behind you…is a room that has not been used in many years. In fact, it may not have been used much in my lifetime." He piqued my curiosity all the more. I needed to find a way in. He shuffled in his pocket and brought out some more keys on a rusty ring. One by one, he slid them on the ring until he seemed to find the one that he had been looking for. I moved aside, realizing what he was doing. With one turn of the key in the lock, he managed to open the door, revealing what looked like it was the largest room in the entire house. Despite there being nothing at all within, the walls and ceiling said it all. Pure white surrounded the room and three lengthy windows in the back echoed light onto the hardwood floors. Gold scrolls of spiral designs framed the windows and trailed around the room, breaking up the white. Two colossal chandeliers that were filled with candles to light hung down from each side of the ceiling, leaving the middle open completely. Looking over at George, it was as though he expected this response from me and wasn't the slightest bit as intrigued as I. He gestured his arm forward as if to tell me to continue walking, and I did just that.

As I treaded forward so that I could stand in the very center of the room, my eyes remained glued to the painting on the ceiling. Unlike the plain simplicity of the walls, the ceiling had hues of blue, beige and various other light shades. When I looked up, it was like a window to the sky above with clouds painted all about and a calming, light blue as the background. The most shocking part of it all were the shades of pink that caused the clouds to look even more realistic than I ever imagined possible to paint. Part of me wanted to gather a sheet from my bed and drape it down in the middle where I stood so that I could lie down and continue staring at its beauty.

"And behold…the ballroom," George snapped me out of my trance-like state. Images flooded my mind of the extravagant gowns that women likely wore to attend balls on this fairytale island that I now called home. Part of me wanted to start twirling around, as I wished I was alone. I would have to plan a ball here at some point. With that thought, an idea popped into my mind. The grand opening. It could be a ball. My eyes sparkled with excitement as to what was to come and all the plans that I could arrange. I continued on through the room and glanced out the middle window, pulling aside the lace sheer that draped down. Although there were quite a few trees in the back, I could clearly see a greenhouse to the right and the ocean's unending waves as they enclosed the entirety of the island.

George followed me as a puppy would to its owner and set a hand on my shoulder of which I jumped again, not expecting it. I should've known by then that he would continue doing that.

"You seem frightened. Has this place already spooked you?" he asked. I felt like he knew something that I didn't, but didn't feel like I could ask him just yet without sounding like a loon. There was something about George that put me on edge, but I couldn't quite place it.

"I'm fine, just getting used to the new place." I gently grasped his fingers and pushed them off my shoulder as I continued through the room to the exit. The next two rooms were nowhere as large as the ballroom had been. There was a very small powder room that could also be used for storage for coats. Adjacent to the powder room was a living area with a wooden table in the center and various red carpets that covered the darker floorboards. This room was much more casual. The ceiling was white, as were the walls, and the only hint of color was that of the golden trims that connected the ceiling with the walls. A few chairs and table were in the very center of the room. What stood out most was the fireplace that was surrounded by large stones, framing its dark depths. I looked over at George in question.

"And you sold this place, why?" I had repeated a question I already asked him, but still couldn't believe the answer he had given me. If I were in his shoes, there would be no way that I'd sell a house of this stature. He shrugged and headed towards the doorway that led back out to the foyer.

"The cooks are likely already making dinner. Perhaps we should meet the others in the dining room?" He changed the subject. My mind jumped to the man that I had seen on the mainland who gave a warning about this island. There must have been more to the story than George might have been willing to reveal, but I wasn't going to let him know about the man I saw. The less he knew, the better. I nodded and politely took his hand as he stood up and led me out of the room. If he was going to play a game, then I would gladly join.

7

With the house came a kitchen staff that I hadn't seen until just now. Surprisingly, they seemed to keep out of our way. George had said that his family often overpaid them so that they would do so. I thought it to be cold and distant, as I wanted to get to know them and help them feel at home. There were two ladies and one man that worked in the kitchen. Both women had their hair back in buns and underneath a white bonnet that tied just below the napes of their necks. One had gray hair while the other had delicate blonde locks. They closely resembled one another, and I wondered if the woman with gray hair was the other's mother. They wore long skirts that a beige tunic was tucked into. The younger woman was much taller than the other and even taller than I, which wasn't saying much since I was of short stature. The man had pale-white skin and wore an apron that was close in color to his face. He was likely the main chef and would send out orders to the others. His face was clean-shaven, and it looked as though he hadn't grown a beard a day in his entire life. His dark hair was kept short and parted a little more than halfway from the middle of his head. It was brushed to the side, and he looked alarmingly serious with his lips in an emotionless crease. A glimpse of his dark eyes was difficult to see since his gaze stayed on his work and never made direct eye contact with anyone, even if they were just entering the room. He primarily stayed in the kitchen while the others frequently came out with servings. George walked over to one of the chairs at the side of the table and pulled it out for me. I made eye contact with him and briefly smiled before taking my seat and promptly being pushed in. The younger maid with blonde hair came over with a pitcher and introduced herself.

"Madam, my name is Alice. My mother, Mary, and I are pleased to serve you this evening." She glanced over at her mother, who had a pitcher at the other side of the table to serve the gentlemen. Alice's face was covered in parades of freckles and her rosy cheeks brought a warmth to the room that it had been missing.

She was the mirror image of her mother if not for the different colored hair and lack of wrinkles.

"Thank you," I sincerely said, and felt a hard nudge at the tip of my foot. As both of our fathers were talking, George silently sat across from me with a devilish smile on his face. I squinted both my eyes at him and furrowed my eyebrows, but he didn't look scared in the slightest. With that, I kicked him back much harder and pulled both my legs back so that they were out of his reach from the other side of the table. After the few seconds that it took him to realize he could no longer reach me, he looked disappointed, and I smiled as this game was fairly won by me.

"Ange, talk to them about our plan for this place!" Father drew our attention away from one another and gladly so. George's father, Charles, looked just as intrigued as his son to hear my plans. I still felt like the place belonged to them and felt awkward talking about it, as it used to be in their family for many generations.

"I haven't explored upstairs enough yet, but I know there are several bedrooms of which we plan to rent out. This could be a vacation home for people and I'm sure they would feel drawn to this place as a mouse is to cheese." I looked over at George, who stifled a laugh at my horrible metaphor and smirked at him.

"There's an extravagant ballroom downstairs as well as this nice dining room. We can have a bed-and-breakfast for our guests that stay in the Charles Island House. Some nights, we will be able to host balls," I looked over at George's father and he surprisingly leaned into the table, interested. I hadn't told father about my last idea, but figured I might as well say it now.

"There will be a grand opening hosted in the ballroom in one week for commoners to attend, as well as a few guests. We can have a prize where we draw a name and those guests will win a free night at the inn." The first part I had come up with when George unlocked the ballroom for me, but the latter idea... I made up as I was speaking to them.

"That's my girl!" Father said and took a long swig of the wine that Mary poured him. I couldn't expect any less from him.

I looked at the others and George was staring at his father with a worried look on his face. It seemed like he didn't know what his response would be, as he was already quite opposed to selling the island in the first place. For the first time, George's father spoke to me.

"You are full of bright ideas, young lady. Your father raised you well," he said and patted Father on the back as he smiled from the praise. The rest of the night was full of laughter as Mary and Alice came in frequently to refill our drinks. They brought out turkey for us to feast on and it was one of the most delicious meals I ever had. On the side were baked potatoes chopped in fourths and some carrots. I was glad that there was a bedroom right upstairs for me since I felt like I could fall asleep right there. When our plates were almost completely cleared off, Alice began collecting them to bring back to the kitchen. We stayed seated and listened to one another's stories. Since George had quite a bit of wine in him, I figured it ought to loosen him up enough to share some information about the island that he looked hesitant to earlier.

"So, is there anything else that we should know about the island?" I asked. I did not want to share my interaction with the man on the mainland that first day we arrived. For some reason, I felt a need to protect him. George looked at his father and when he gave him a nod, it looked as though he was allowing him to answer me. He rolled his shoulders back and began.

"We have kept this house in our family for a while, but it was sold to us by a plantation owner. After we fixed it up, we started staying here and calling it our vacation home. It has been a great house that we were fortunate to have, but as Father has retired and I am occupied with work, it only made sense to sell it." He breathed out and checked in with his father once again.

It was as though he was sugar-coating whatever he was about to say next. In any case, it would be too late for us to back out of the deal we had made with them.

"At night, there would sometimes be strange occurrences that we couldn't really explain. It was likely just some deer or other creatures, but you'll be fine as long as you just stay inside," he said, as if it were no big deal. I felt my eyebrows furrow up in question. He was definitely leaving out a lot, but now wasn't the time to ask, with both of our fathers staring intently.

"Well, Ange! You heard them! Just stay inside like you would have anyway," Father grunted as he tried to get up out of his seat to walk them out.

"Wait, have you seen the chef again? I wanted to thank him for the delicious meal!" I asked. Everyone looked dumbfounded, including the two maids who were gathering our empty glasses and plates.

"Madam, *we* made the meal for you," Alice said. Her mother walked over to me and smiled.

"It's okay, perhaps a little bit too much to drink," she chuckled and took the half-full glass of wine away from me. It was odd because I could have sworn I saw a man with an apron on that stayed in the kitchen as a chef...

"You ought to stay away from the wine," George repeated back, mockingly. I gave him a gentle push on his shoulder.

"I should be walking you out now, shouldn't I?" I asked, unable to get him out soon enough. He seemed to try to be charming, but was also like an annoying brother. Although I never had any siblings, I imagined it to feel like this.

Just when we were about to get to the door, Father turned around toward us and put his arm around Charles as if they had known one another forever.

"Where are my manners?! It is just about to reach dusk and you both would have a long ways to go in the boat. Why don't you stay in one of the guest rooms upstairs?!" he suggested, to my surprise.

No...Way... This wasn't happening. George smiled the biggest smile I had seen on him all along, like he was a child in a candy shop.

"That's a great idea, Mr. Williams!" George shouted. His father seemed to agree as they headed back in.

"Oh, call me John! Let's go to the living space and we'll have some warm tea before bed," he noted. I rolled my eyes, unable to protest against this ridiculous idea Father had. I had to find some way out of the remaining activities.

"I'm going to head upstairs to sleep. I'll be in the main bedroom in the front, okay?" I said.

"You alright, Ange?" Father asked. I nodded and waved to George and his father. Upon turning around, I smiled, as I had won a second time and was able to get away. As I headed up the grand staircase, I did not turn to look back at them, but knew they were busy from the laughter I heard. It lingered as it trailed into the living space, which was the room adjacent to the ballroom. As I continued walking around the banister and to the front, I noticed how square-like everything was. When I got to the main bedroom in the front of the house, I turned the knob and was met with the same awful lock as I had with the ballroom door. I clenched my jaw, knowing I would have to go back downstairs to get the key from George… why hadn't he given us all of those keys, anyway? They should've come with the main keys to the house. Before I could head back downstairs, he was already wandering up with the keys around the ring, shaking it as if he had won a prize. I crossed my arms over my chest and followed him as he unlocked the door to the bedroom.

In The Night

8

All was still in the night; the only light being that of the moon as it cast its reflection through the steady flow of the ocean. A cool breeze sent a chilling whisper down my spine as I found myself wandering through the land. From the distance, I could see the mainland as the waters gently drifted up its sandy shores. A pathway leading from the mainland to the very spot that I stood was tempting as part of me wanted to venture back home to the place that I felt most secure and safe. I turned around to face the house and found there to be an encapsulating darkness. No one must have heard me as I crept outside, but for some reason I didn't remember venturing out anywhere in the first place. I began walking toward the house so that I could go back to sleep when I saw a glimmer of light other than the moon that had previously been the sole illumination in the night. This glow was much more distinct to one location as it shone out just past the trees on the left side of the house. Wondering if it was Father or one of our other guests, I turned in that direction. There was an outhouse just a few yards away from the main house…so it could have very well been one of our guests.

"Hello?" I called out, breaking the silence. I continued using the moon as a focal point, but also followed the fiery glow, as a fly would be drawn to a light. There was something strange about whomever lurked within the night. It was almost as if they had been carrying a lantern with them, but couldn't seem to see or hear me. I tried calling out a second time to them, but still…nothing. As I drew closer, I was able to make out a tall figure in the distance. It appeared to be a man with work clothes on, which was another strange occurrence since the day had come to an end. Ignoring me as if he were unable to hear me at all, he continued walking toward the farthest point of the island. The path to the mainland was beginning to wash up and caused me to become all the more anxious. *I shouldn't be out here. I need to go back.*

Nevertheless, I continued on — unable to give into the gut feeling that I had of an inevitable disturbance. I looked down at what I was wearing and saw I still had the dress on from earlier that I used while entertaining the guests that had joined us for our feast. The bottom of the dress was soaking wet and so I grasped a bunch on each side to continue walking without ruining it further. Through the trees in the back of the house, I continued following the light. As I drew closer, I felt I could almost hear a humming. It continued and only grew louder… As the repetitive melody filled my ears, I finally remembered it from one of the nursery rhymes mother used to sing to me. He was humming "Mary Had a Little Lamb," except the way in which he sang it sent chills down my spine just as much as the cool breeze had. The fact that he was all by himself while humming this tune that a grown man normally would not be doing in the first place made it even more displaced. As he reached the edge of the island, just as the waters washed up on these shores…he stopped abruptly and stared out. It looked like he was in some sort of trance. Placing a hand on each of his hips, he continued staring into the blankness that night was. From the foolish song to the uneasiness that roared in my stomach, I continued calling out to him.

"Hey, you're going to get sick. Come back in!" I called out. With this final attempt, he seemed to hear me, which meant that he might have heard me the entire time and only just ignored my words. He glanced my way, and that is when I was able to make out exactly who he was. Only this time, he smiled…an eery smile that a person only wore when they were up to something mischievous. Unlike when I saw him previously, his hair was now disheveled, as if he had been running his fingers through it again and again. The front of his work clothes that he wore were concealed by a kitchen apron. The chef. Before I could say anything else, his smile faded to a frown, and he turned his entire body to face the water again. Without further delay, he began walking into the water despite being fully clothed.

"What are you doing?! Stop!!" I screamed. He didn't seem to care as he continued and was already neck-deep. I didn't know how to swim, otherwise I would have gone in after him. My begging didn't seem to matter as he continued on until his head was fully submerged and the only remnants were a few bubbles that traveled up to the water's surface. My heart pounded in my chest as I ran to find help. At first, I made it to the back door of the house and pulled and pulled on the handle, only to be met with nothing in turn as it was locked. I tried a door on the side of the house and still, there was no luck. My last shot was the front door, which was sure to be open since that was the way I had come. When I turned the handle, my heart sank as it didn't open either. I pounded my fists into the door as hard as I could, again and again, hoping that someone would hear me and they could come help the man who just seemed to have drowned himself.

"Please, somebody!!! Help!" I shouted out, tears streaming down my cheeks. In that moment, I felt more alone than I ever had in my entire life. There was no one to turn to or lean on. I was completely isolated. I turned and saw that the pathway to the mainland was just washing up. If I ran, I still had time. I tore off each of my shoes and threw them to the side, not thinking about the sharp shells that lined the path — but instead, just surviving the night. As I picked up each side of my dress in my hands, I began to run as fast as I could towards the mainland. I bit my lip in pain as the various shells and rocks dug into the soles of my feet. There was something calling me home and away from the wretched island that seemed to be a prize by looking at the outside but couldn't have been more deceiving. My eyes blurred as I cried from the pain, but also pure horror of what I had just witnessed. Who was that man? Why had no one else seen him but me? Where was everyone in the house? I continued on, feeling as if the pathway was the longest stretch I had ever run on in my entire life.

I was just about to reach the shore of the mainland when I noticed a familiar face that I had seen before.

And although it was of someone I barely met, I couldn't have been more glad to see another living soul on the mainland. Having someone else there…anyone there…proved that I was, in fact, not completely alone. The darkness that had swept up the entire world with me inside was less frightening when someone was at least by my side. I ran into his arms and hugged him as tight as I could, feeling as if I had known him for much longer. The length of his thick, black hair dangled over my shoulders as he held me in a firm embrace that I didn't ever want to leave. After a few moments, he began to pull away from me. Out of great reluctance not to let go, I pulled him closer and was barely able to reach my arms completely around his stocky build. As I placed my hands on his bare skin, I felt a warmth that I needed. It was a protection that suddenly made me feel safer despite the horror that had just happened. He held me for a moment longer and pulled away, staring straight into my eyes with the same look that he had given me when I saw him on the mainland with the fawn. The same look of worry spread across his face as he had when he warned me not to go to the island in the first place. I felt his hand as it gently touched my cheek to wipe my tears away. In that moment, I felt as if there was nothing to fear as long as he was by my side. He said two words that seemed to echo through my mind.

"Come back."

As soon as he pulled me back into his body, enveloping his robust arms around me, the night encompassed all around me as the world suddenly went black.

Stranger

9

I woke up with the worst headache of my life; all light that was let in from the curtains made it even more difficult to keep my eyes open. I pulled the covers over my head and hid, hoping to be left alone for at least a while longer.

"Madam, breakfast is ready downstairs," the familiar voice of the younger maid called out. I heard her opening the curtains even more-so than before, letting an abundance of light in.

"Tell them I'm still sleeping," I groaned, having no desire whatsoever to put on an act for George and his father. I squeezed my eyes and began rubbing my temples, suddenly overwhelmed in deep confusion. I had somehow found myself to bed, but felt like I hadn't slept a wink. My entire body hurt as if I had been running miles and miles the night before. As I sat up in bed, the blanket that I had previously used as a shield from the burning sunlight fell to my lap. Alice was still in the room and appeared to be gathering things in my wardrobe. Normally, I would have made a fuss about someone else rummaging through my things, but there were more pressing thoughts in my mind.

"Come, you should get dressed," she attempted again. With a long sigh, I reached my arms up to stretch and then fell back into the comfort of the pillow filled with down feathers. She left the dress that had been in her hands on the vanity and walked to my bedside, arms crossed. This lady didn't seem to take no for an answer. She would have to learn…

"Are you feeling alright, Lady Angeline?" she asked, feeling my forehead for warmth. "You've been in bed since early last night. In fact, you were the first to enter your chambers." This was certainly news to me, as the last thing I remembered was…

"Were there any other people who ever worked here?" I asked, wishing I could take my words back as soon as I said them. Of course, there were other workers…it was a question that I already knew the answer to.

"Yes," she nodded and walked back over towards the vanity to retrieve the dress. I distinctly remembered the two men from my dream. The first made me shudder just thinking about him, but I was sure that he worked on this island at some point. I had seen him in the kitchen and then…last night. It could have just been a dream, though. That would have made more sense.

"A man that wore an apron and worked in the kitchen, perhaps? He had dark brown hair and no beard or mustache whatsoever." I gave more details, hoping to jog her memory. If she worked on the island, she had to have run into him at some point. To my surprise, she stopped dead in her tracks as if I bore the worst news possible to her. As her eyebrows furrowed up, I could tell she was likely almost as confused as I currently was. Anyone else that had never heard of the man before would've just kept going about their business. But the fact that at first mention, she looked like she was hit by a bag of bricks, it revealed that she must have at least heard of him.

"How do you know of him?" she asked. Aside from being in the kitchen the other day, he was also in my dream, but I couldn't tell her of that part...not yet, at least.

"I thought I saw him in the kitchen, or maybe it was a photograph in the living space downstairs," I said, ensuring to be careful with every word I said. Alice finished walking the distance to the bed and sat at the very end as I still sat up, unable to find the energy to walk on my legs quite yet. It looked as though a brief sadness washed over her face. I could have sworn a tear streamed down her cheek as she carefully wiped it away and looked back at me with a friendly smile, masking whatever feelings she previously had.

"It sounds like James. James was our head chef here years ago and boy, was he extraordinary at his work. From the very start, we were all hired together…we've been here since George was just a young boy," she sighed, as if reminiscing on better days.

"Everything that I do in the kitchen, I've learned from James. We each had our own bedrooms that we'd sleep in right here at the island house. George's family was so good to us and would even invite us to the dining table, joining them at the various feasts and parties they held." She stopped and gestured me to come over to the vanity and get dressed. Since she was opening up with all the information that I sought, listening to her was the least I could do. As she handed me the dress, I went behind the changing wall and slipped out of my nightgown.

"Then what happened?" I asked, coming out from behind the wall so that she could tighten the laces on the back of the dress. It would be impossible for me to get in and out of this without someone like her. And because of that, it became an imprisonment in a way.

"Strange things happened in the night and George's family stopped staying here. This became a place that they would only visit," she noted and on the last pull of the ribbons, I took a deep breath in and felt like I couldn't exhale all the way. She seemed to notice as she undid the last knot she made and loosened it a bit.

"But then, why did they stay here last night?" I asked the obvious question.

"They didn't," she was quick to answer. "After you went to bed, they had more to drink, then left to head back to the mainland." It was news to me. Here I thought I'd have to creep around the house, steering clear of George.

"So...what happened to James?" I circled back around to my original question. It was like pulling teeth trying to get this answer out of her. It seemed like she wanted to tell me about anything else but him, and I wasn't sure why. I walked over to the vanity and sat down, fumbling through the drawers to see which jewelry I wanted to wear.

"Come, come," she said, tugging at my arm and led me to the opposite side of the room where another vanity stood, looking much more expensive than the one I had. Sitting at the stool to this vanity, I was afraid to go through any of the drawers as nothing belonged to me. Alice went on ahead and opened up the drawer closest to her, revealing several necklaces...far more than I had ever seen in my life.

"These don't belong to me," I said, unsure of whose collection this was. Alice ignored my response and took out a gold necklace that was interwoven like a braid, meeting in the middle with a blood-red gem. She opened up a smaller drawer above the one she previously rummaged through and took out matching earrings. The blood-red was a similar shade to the dining room and also the dress she had chosen for me to wear that day, which I had never seen before, either.

"These belong to George's mother. Everything in this house is now yours to do with what you wish," she said as she handed me the necklace. I gently touched it with my fingertips. It felt cold and unused, but did match everything else I was wearing perfectly.

"Thank you. I think I am going to wear something lighter today, though. It's late summer and this would be better off worn in the winter," I said.

"Good point!" She scurried over and grabbed some lighter clothes from the wardrobe.

"Ok, let me tell you about James... Swear that you won't tell anyone, okay?" She requested urgently. I nodded, and she placed another outfit on my lap so that I could walk over to the changing wall to put it on instead.

"The maids and other workers stayed here in the house, awaiting the family's visits. It seemed like a great deal since we pretty much had the house to ourselves, if only for the upkeep, which wasn't terrible. James stayed upstairs in a room in the attic, which is sealed off now. My mother and I stayed in these rooms here on the second floor. Sometimes, we would switch from room to room due to boredom. Anyway, something seemed to change in James. He would often go out at night and give no explanation as to why or what he would be doing. All he said to us was to make sure that we stayed in the house with the doors locked, whatever we did. Mother and I both thought that he was just keeping guard and protecting us. One night, there was a bit of a scream from outside and I rushed to the back room on the second floor, which is where your father is staying. As I peered out the window, I could see him in the distance. I continued out onto the balcony so as to take a better look, keeping in mind the fact that we were not allowed to exit the house so late at night." She paused and breathed in and out a few times as if she were calming herself. She looked at me in the mirror's reflection and stopped combing my hair, focusing fully on the conversation.

"I can remember that night very vividly, as if it was just yesterday. He was fully clothed and walking straight into the waters until…his entire body was submerged and I could no longer see him. I screamed for mother and she rushed over to me, forbidding me to go out there and check on him. You see, there were rumors of dangerous creatures in the night that lurked on this island. But I didn't care in that moment. All I cared about was going out there to get him and bring him back in," she said as she began sobbing uncontrollably. I grabbed a handkerchief that lay on the vanity and handed it to her, pulling her close into a hug and rubbed her back as I remembered Mother would for me when I was just a young girl.

"I'm sorry." She pulled away, cheeks red with embarrassment. "I shouldn't have lost my wits. I just…" She breathed in heavily, trying to slow each breath one at a time, then continued, "I miss him so much. He and I were bound to get married someday." Unsure of what to say, I tried to think of the words that people said to me when I had lost my mother.

"He's in a better place, Alice. It's okay," I said, knowing that anything I said would never bring him back or make it better for her. But the simple task of trying to comfort her was something I knew I had to do. She blew her nose into the handkerchief and took the seat at the vanity that I had previously been sitting in.

"Just…don't go out at night, okay? And all will be well," she reminded me, looking up with horror in her eyes.

Venturing

10

Unlike the last time that I had gone into the kitchen, there was no sign of the man. Part of me felt relieved while the other left with even more questions. Just before I left my room, I went into the vanity and took out my journal so that I could bring it with me on my journey outside today. I had placed it in a satchel and draped it over my shoulder. When I entered the kitchen, Alice's mother, Mary, was cutting bread that she had just baked in the oven. Her earnest smile upon my entering the room seemed forced as she quickly got back to her work. As I passed the fruit bowl, I grabbed an apple then continued to leave the kitchen.

"Wait, you're going to have to eat more than that," Mary called after me. I turned toward her and saw that she was gathering a few slices of bread to hand to me. Today's plan was to venture out on the property since I couldn't during the night. It was much less daunting to take it on when the sun was still out.

"I'll come back. I'm going to walk around outside for a bit." I smiled and took a huge bite out of the side of the apple as the juices seeped out. Before I could turn back around, I noticed she was still persisting in giving me the bread as she wrapped it up and put it into a wooden basket that had a braided handle on it.

"Here, just take it with you in case you get hungry." She plopped another apple into the basket. This reminded me much of my mother and how she would always look out for me in a comforting, but overbearing way. I missed it.

"Thanks Mary." I took the basket and headed out of the kitchen and through the dining room. All was untouched, as if we hadn't feasted there previously. There wasn't the slightest hint of living as it looked like it had when I first entered the home. Dishes out on the table with a setting of forks and knives to accompany them. Handkerchiefs beside each plating and various glasses about the table.

"Ange?! You in there??" Father hollered from the office.

"Yes, Father?" I called back and followed his voice to find him exactly where I thought he'd be. He stood beside the desk, hovering over several papers and a feather pen dipped in ink. He was rereading a letter that he had already written.

"I'm going into town to deliver this news," he said as he grabbed his satchel and started piling in various items. He began to roll the letter up. "Oh, the ink may not be dry!" He unrolled it, revealing smears of what used to be handwritten words.

"What's the rush?" I asked, gathering another paper and dipping the pen into the ink so that I could help him rewrite the ruined one.

"We have to spread the news of our grand opening. Your job is to organize the event here on the island, but George and his father are waiting out on their boat to escort me back to the mainland." He set the other paper beside me so I could quickly copy it in a neater form. As I copied, I also skimmed the words to gain the information he had clearly planned out this morning while I had been talking with Alice. After the first few words, I could barely make out the rest.

"Can you read it to me while I write?" I asked, unable to decipher the remaining smears of ink. Father set his satchel down and huffed, frustrated as he had been in a rush.

"George is waiting out there. Maybe I can just write it once I get there," he explained.

"Nonsense, they can wait," I assured him. That seemed to have won him over quite easily.

"Ok, ok...what have you got so far?" He peered over at the introduction to the letter and started with that. I got the pen ready to write away. "GRAND OPENING!" He exclaimed as excited as it looked down on paper. "Charles Island House welcomes you to the first ever ball at our inn! Enroll in the raffle upon entering to win a complimentary stay with breakfast the morning thereafter. August 20, 1849 — 6:00PM at Charles Island House — take your boat and dock on the shores of this beautiful, luxurious island." He finished, and it felt as though he added more to the end, since the previous letter wasn't nearly as long.

"Be careful," I said as I handed him the letter. "Oh, and don't roll this one up quite yet." I smirked at him and he rolled his eyes as he tapped me on the head. I felt like one of those dogs when their owners say "good boy" and taps them on the head. He knew I hated it and that just caused him to find it all the more amusing when I rolled my eyes.

"Wish me luck!" He blurted out, and I helped him to his satchel and other items he planned to bring along with him.

"Good luck, I love you!" I called out and in the next moment, he was out the door heading towards the paddle boat that belonged to George and his father. I was careful not to peek my head out so that George wouldn't catch sight of me. That was the last thing I needed today — this was a day that I would spend by myself, learning what else the island had in store for me.

Once there was no sight of anyone around the house, I crept out the back door with my satchel draped over my shoulder. Today, I didn't dress up as much since there weren't any visitors expected and I didn't plan to go into town either. I wore a light blue sunhat that had a matching ribbon in the back that Alice tied. An opaque blouse covered my torso and was tied by various strings in the back. A long, light blue skirt went down to my ankles, concealing my feet. The sunhat was a nice touch, as the sun was almost blinding outside. As soon as I stepped out, I had to squint while my eyes adjusted to the light. A path went straight from the back door to the beach and the coast of the island was lined with several places to dock. From here, there were many trees that towered over the inn. If it weren't for the path, I wouldn't have been able to see down toward the docks. I decided to follow it, as the waters always seemed to calm me. Being just about anywhere on the island, I could feel a cooling breeze no matter how hot the day was, it seemed. I knew I could definitely get used to it. My thoughts whirled around all the planning

I would have to do for the grand opening, but for some reason, I couldn't focus on it, as other wonders puzzled me. As the crashing waves smoothed out into bubbly shallows above the sandy surface, I walked as close as I could without getting wet. Several rocks covered the sandy shores, and I picked the flattest to sit on. I was thankful for the satchel that father had given me many years ago because my journal fit perfectly within. A day to go write was a day well spent to me. As soon as I opened up the notebook, a strong breeze flipped the pages for me toward the very end and the last page revealed itself. It was in my mother's handwriting.

Angeline,

If you are reading this, you've made it through the journal I left you all those years ago. I had a feeling that I wouldn't be around to say this to you since the sickness came on, but I want you to know that no matter what, I am incredibly proud of the person you are. Even if you do nothing else in this world, you've brought so much light into my life as well as your father's. We each come into this world alone, but learn more about those that gave life to us. And through that, we love one another unconditionally. Ever since you were little and sought to adventure all day and explore new things as opposed to playing with your hair like the other girls, you were so different and unique. I want you to know that I am here for you and I will stay with you always. You may see the simplest of signs that I *am here and I want you to cherish those times just as I*

cherish the memories you have given me.

Love,

Mom

Before I could help it, a tear streamed down my cheek and fell onto the paper, partly smudging the word "Love." I felt as though my heart was racing endlessly and at any second, it would surely jump out of my chest. I wanted more than anything just to talk to her again. I decided to close the book and just look out at the water. It seemed that the tide was going down since the water receded away from where it had been before. Looking out at the ocean's vast beauty left me staring a while longer. A sudden flash of black drifted by me and I looked all around to figure out what it was from. Nothing. I stood up and shoved the journal back into my satchel, continuing to look around when it landed on the rock I had just been sitting on.

It was a blackbird that didn't seem frightened in the slightest by my presence. As it perched on the rock, it seemed to be looking at me. A small hint of orange peeked out from each wing, causing me to wonder how it would appear when it took flight. This was the closest I had ever been to a bird, since they would normally fly away at the sight of a person. As I crept toward it, it hopped back and forth a few times, then jumped up in the air, soaring above me with its wings fully extended. On each was a small patch of orange, outlined in yellow. It looked as though its wings had been painted. It flew toward the side of the house, heading for the front. I followed, curious as to where it was going and also feeling like a fool, but glad that no one was around to watch.

From the front, it perched on a tree right next to the entrance of the inn. I carried my skirt up so as not to get it dirty and cocked my head to the side.

"Little bird, why aren't you scared of me?" I asked aloud, as if it could understand me. It took flight again and headed toward the sandy path that led to the mainland, continuing all the way down. I followed.

11

The delirious bird that drove me even more insane brought me all the way to the mainland where I had first stood when I saw the island with Father. As soon as I reached the shores, it had disappeared from view as if its mission was accomplished. The waves crashed behind me and as I looked at the island from farther away; it appeared that much smaller. I began walking back toward the island when I heard something rustling in the distance. The day seemed to be getting even more puzzling as it went on. I should've never left the bed... As the water sloshed over shells again and again, a seaweed path lined just above all the shells. I walked more inland and carefully stepped over the slimy green boundary when I heard the rustling again. A brown fawn stepped out of the bushes and its ears were raised up intently, clearly startled by my presence. I began walking toward it more slowly. Its dark brown back was freckled with white dots starting at its shoulders. It was a much lighter shade of brown which matched its face. Its eyes were dark, as was its nose. Directly under its mouth was pure white. It was completely still, as if frozen to the core. I didn't want to scare it so I started backing off a bit, not looking behind me as I wanted to keep my eyes on the cutest creature I had ever laid eyes on. It looked vaguely familiar to the fawn that seemed to belong to the man who warned me about the island. I continued backing up until I couldn't any longer and hit something that felt as stiff as a tree that I could've sworn was not there before.

"Hi," it spoke. Someone must have slipped me something, maybe opium…in my drink this morning. First the bird, then the fawn and now…I turned around to find the Native man that I had seen on the mainland before. I was remarkably close to him, but my chin only came up to his chest as he towered over me. As I backed up a bit, he mirrored me and walked toward the fawn. Its ears were down and it didn't seem as frightened by him as it was of me. He started petting its side as one would stroke a horse.

"It's ok, Kitchi," he said, reassuring it as if it was a pet of his. I just watched him in shock, silently accepting the fact that yes, it was very likely that I had been given opium. Nothing concealed the upper half of his body as his broad shoulders showed how muscular he was. His skin was much darker than mine and had a rosy tint to it, full of warmth. I noticed a scar that went from his neck diagonally down to the middle of his back. I wondered what had hurt him and how he would've even survived a wound as big as that. He turned back toward me and I fidgeted, still trying to back away from the strange man. I had no idea what he was capable of; let alone if he would let me leave.

"She is scared of your people. They hunt her kind without giving back," he said. I had never been hunting, but did enjoy venison. I felt sick to my stomach thinking about having possibly eaten this young fawn's family and instantly pressed my hand against my abdomen. He continued on, "I found Kitchi alone and she has followed me around ever since. Kitchi means brave because she was able to survive even without her family." He seemed more interested in telling me about the fawn, as if it were a good friend of his. I had never seen anything like it before.

"Well, she doesn't need to be afraid of me," I said, silently vowing never to eat venison again. "I don't hunt." I crept closer toward him and the fawn. I figured if this stranger were going to hurt me, it would've already happened. There was a softness to him that made me feel like I could trust him. As the basket I held swayed back and forth with every step I took, I decided to place it down and was struck with an idea upon looking at it.

"That is a very good idea. She loves apples." His beaming smile shone out against his darkened skin as I stood back up with the apple in my hand that Mary had given me earlier.

"Here, put your hand out first," he requested as he continued rubbing her side. She backed up slightly, still unsure of me. "Shh, shh…it's ok" he said to her, and she stopped backing up. When I finally reached her while still holding my hand out, he looked into my eyes as if to gain permission to take my hand in his and led me just in front of her mouth so that she could sniff the apple. She initially backed up, but curiosity won her over and as soon as she took one sniff of the apple, she took one small bite out of the side and began chomping on the sweet treat. I continued holding it for her as she took more bites, one by one. When she finished and the core was the only thing that remained, she attempted at biting that too and the man took it out of my hands and just started laughing.

"You don't eat that part, silly," he exclaimed. I wanted to pet her, but felt that I would just scare her even more. He seemed to read my mind and took my hand, leading me just below her chin to gently rub her. Gradually, his warm grasp left my hand, and I was just stroking her on my own. When I woke up that morning, I would have never guessed I would be petting a baby deer and here I was with this person I still didn't know by name.

"Who are you?" I finally asked, still petting her as it seemed to calm her down.

"Calian...you can call me Cal." He started walking toward the shore and went straight through the seaweed that I had so carefully avoided. "What about you?"

"Angeline. But my father calls me Ange," I replied. I had so many questions for him and for some reason, I felt safe even though I hadn't really met him before. If Father caught me on the mainland with him, he'd likely find some way to lock me up in the house so that I could never leave again. That, or he would send me to a convent. Although he looked rigid on the outside, there was a gentle side to him. This time, he didn't have any arrows in a bag over his shoulder. The only thing covering him were long brown slacks that seemed to blend in with the earth around him.

"That's a beautiful name," he remarked.

"Thank you. What does your name mean?" I asked, remembering the distinct meaning of Kitchi's name. It seemed there was a purpose for everything they named in their language. He turned around and crossed his arms over his chest.

"Warrior of life," he replied simply. It made sense as he protected the little fawn and likely did the same with other creatures. I walked closer toward him and peered out at the island as he just had.

"How do you know how to speak my language?" It was confusing because I knew the Natives had a language of their own yet rarely saw them out in public.

"When the settlers came in, they tried to assimilate us," he revealed and sighed. "We had to change a lot of our culture in order to fit in. Some customs, we have kept the same. My tribe used to own the territory along the coastline…" I could tell that he was deeply troubled by the history of his people.

"Why, what happened?" I asked, desperate to know more. While the other girls were busy finding suitors, I was always immersed in books. History was something that truly fascinated me, and I always yearned to know more about other cultures.

"We needed protection from a neighboring tribe and sold a lot of our land to the settlers in order to gain that protection. Our people were pushed into a difficult position that haunts us to this day," he replied grimly. My heart went out to him and although I didn't know who he was exactly, I felt pressed to give him a hug but stayed back, unsure.

Without having to ask anymore questions, he seemed to read my mind. "There is a curse on the land out there. I was trying to warn you not to go there, but

I guess it is too late," he sighed and turned back toward the island, shaking his head.

"What is the curse?" I asked, curiosity piqued. I had a feeling I knew more than he thought I did.

"Have you ever heard of someone's spirit staying when they had unfinished work in their lifetime?" I shook my head, confused. "Forget it. You won't believe me, anyway." He gave up too soon, but I would have felt the same if I were in his position. If I hadn't seen what I had the other night, I would've been very skeptical of the story he was telling. He began walking back toward Kitchi. She had stayed next to the bush, feasting on some of its leaves. I quickly followed him and grabbed his arm to stop him from leaving.

"No, I have seen things…things that I cannot explain. Please tell me," I requested. He seemed surprised as he looked down at my hand that was on his arm. I released my hold on him and stared straight into his chestnut brown eyes.

"Well, the evil spirits lay trapped on the island…sometimes they take the form of a beast…sometimes they look like a regular person," he explained as he sat on a rock. "My tribe lost so much to the creature that lurked on its land. We tried to warn many people of this, but no one usually listens…" he sighed. I walked in front of him, at which point he put his head in his hands, frustrated.

"There is this man that I could have sworn I saw during dinner, but no one else seemed to see him… and then at night, I watched as he drowned himself. Well…it was a dream because you were there. But it felt so real." I felt a weight lift off my shoulders when I revealed what I saw. I had been holding it in for longer than I felt possible. He looked back up at me, stern and full of worry.

"You need to stay away from there," he warned and gently took each of my wrists in his hands.

"But there is no way…my father won't ever sell the inn and now I have to prepare for its grand opening." I suddenly felt full of regret. The only thing that I wanted to do was abandon the inn and go back to where I once lived with Father. Button-making was redundant, but I would've taken that life over one of horror and malice. Cal must have felt the concern in my tone as he stood up and held me tight to his chest in a hug. His arms wrapped around my back fully as I felt like a toothpick in his grasp.

"We will figure out a way…for now, just do not go out at night," he said. Kitchi took off in an instant and we heard voices coming from nearby, one of which belonged to my father.

"Quick, run so they don't see you!" I whispered. Cal took the order without question and disappeared into the bushes along with the fawn. My heart was racing even more than it had been previously, but this time, in fear of being found with a man that was highly frowned upon during these times. I sat on the rock that Cal had just been on and wished we had more time. As I stayed there, I waited for them and their voices became louder, signaling that they drew closer. Their paddle boat was up on the shores nearby, so they would surely take it to go back to the island.

"Ange?!" Father called out, just as surprised as I was to be here on the mainland again. "How did you get all the way over here?" George followed closely behind, but ran over to me and took my hand. I just looked out toward the bushes where Cal had gone. I felt deceived by George because he must have known that the island held a curse. It all made sense now why his family never actually lived in the house and only used it to come to time and time again as a beach house. It was no use to explain anything because it was very likely that they would just call me crazy.

"I'm ok, I'm ok — just walked down the path and found myself over here," I answered, taking George's hand and standing up beside them. Father grabbed the picnic basket that I had placed down earlier and opened it up, helping himself to some bread. It made me happy how comfortable he was to do things like that. It was not very common for a daughter to have a close relationship with her father, let alone be a business partner.

"We'll bring you back in the boat, okay?" George said, seemingly kissing up in front of Father. Something about him was very off, and it seemed like there was an ulterior motive behind his actions.

"That's fine." I forced a smile and got in the paddle boat with them, ensuring not to say a word. I made a mental note to tell Father later about the warnings of going out at night. If anything happened to him, I'd be done.

Planning

12

The entire ride, no matter how hard I tried to avoid George, he seemed all the more drawn to me. I even got a few looks from Father after his not-so-subtle attempts at flirting. Compliments about my appearance, requests to walk the beach with me sometime and talk about his upcoming ventures in life… it didn't interest me in the slightest. All I kept thinking about was Calian, who was different from any other man I had met. If I were to end up with George, I would be in the same rut that most women found themselves in. A shiny, new toy at first and once children came into the picture…I would be nothing but a maid with not much of a point in my life. But Calian, on the other hand…there was no knowing what life would be like and that would be adventure enough. Uncertainty can be a great discomfort to most, but the thrill of the unknown would be worth every second. It was uncommon for our people to mingle with theirs…let alone be with. In fact, it was frowned upon in every way and wouldn't be allowed. I didn't see the reason why, as Calian showed his kindness even to the most vulnerable of creatures in a time when no one was looking. I feel that our actions behind closed doors speak the most about who we truly are. People like George do things in front of others to impress them and

I just couldn't see him having the same kind nature. Society had a way of setting boundaries to the point that he would be my suitable mate, though. I hated it.

"So, let's talk about this grand opening. Guests would be thrilled to enter a raffle; having the possibility of winning a free stay. I think that's a great idea," George kissed up. The mirage seemed to be working on Father since he nodded and smiled at me, also awaiting a response.

"Yes, people love free things and I figured it would help to bring more guests in," I answered, unsure of the plan I had come up with as the night was the most uncertain time of all...I looked off at the waves as they pressed up against the boat and retreated back in a bubbly clash.

"I can help you plan, you know? We can only come here in the day, though," George suggested. I was just about to open up my mouth to refuse when Father replied instead.

"That would be great! I felt bad leaving most of it to Ange, but you know the ins and outs of this place so your help would be much appreciated," he assured him. I couldn't help the frown that peeled over my face and looked back out at the waters, toward the mainland, aggravated. The boat ride with him was just enough…now our time together would have to go on even longer. It also didn't make sense how he could only come during the day.

"I'm free all day today. How about we go inside and get started?" George insisted, breaking my gaze back toward where Calian had just been with me. *It would make Father happy...*

"It's a plan," I said as I bit my lip, nearly causing it to bleed. He just smiled along with my father, both clearly oblivious to my true feelings. The paddle boat reached the shores of the island and it was about midday, so there was still a good amount of time until the darkness enveloped the sky. As he had earlier, he gave my father a hand first to help him out and then reached his hand out to me. I slightly pulled up the light blue skirt that I had been wearing and reached out for his hand to make the gentle leap from the boat to the sandy shores. When I looked straight at him, he smiled and I avoided eye contact from there on. Ahead, father was already in a rush to get back in the house as he left us trailing behind.

"You all get on with the planning. I'll be upstairs in my room sorting finances," Father called back without even the slightest glance back at us. I silently hoped that Father would have joined us in one of the rooms and not leave us completely alone, but it didn't look like that was happening.

George walked beside me the rest of the way and boasted on and on about his most recent endeavors as a banker. It seemed never ending.

"The other day, you wouldn't believe what happened! I managed to save the bank so much money by ensuring that we give a loan out to one man over the other who would have never been able to pay us back! He even brought some of his associates to do banking with us as well," George blabbed on.

"Oh, wow…" I said, disinterested, but he didn't seem to tell in the slightest. After telling me about the endeavors, there was an awkward silence as we headed into the house. Normally, Father would be in the office, but this time he was upstairs hiding away, which is where I would have very much liked to have been.

"So, where shall we plan for this grand opening?" I asked, ensuring that we stay on task. He was heading toward the back of the house on the left-hand side of the main floor, and I could tell he already knew where we would be going.

"Let's go to the living room space; it is a nice place to discuss things," George explained his reasoning for heading to the left. I agreed and would've likely chosen the same place.

"That's a good plan. I'm going to head into the office real quick to collect some papers so we can write this down," I said and scurried over toward the office that Father had been in this morning. Just as I expected, the papers and feather pen were in the same exact place as they had been when he and I both left. Sealing the container of ink, I carried the remaining things back with me to the living room. In my short absence, George had opened the curtains to draw in the sun so we wouldn't have to light any candles. He looked back over at me from the farthest window and I could have sworn I saw him draw his eyes up and down my body.

"Perfect," he said and snapped himself out of it, walking over to the table to pull out a chair for me like the perfect gentleman that he was… I set out a stack of papers on either side of the table so that we would each have some and put the ink in the very center. He took his seat across from me and handed the feather pen over, first dipping it in ink.

"You're going to want to write this down…" he explained as I took the pen and wondered what he could have possibly come up with already.

"August 20, 1849 - 6:00pm - GRAND OPENING," he repeated the same first line that had been in the letter I copied for Father. I wrote the date and time so the notes could at least have a title of some sort.

"I know this," I said, hesitantly. "It's a shame we are having it at night…" I couldn't express my uncertainty of the issue more.

"When the night comes, people can leave… Not a problem." He was quick to ease my worries, which he probably thought he did, but hadn't at all.

"Okay, so it will be in the ballroom. We need a plan for this and also include some information about the food that will be present," I said, coming up with more items for my to-do list as I continued to think.

"One thing at a time," he assured me. "Let's talk about the ballroom first. There is a closet on the left-hand side that can store people's coats and various things, such as luggage, that they will not need in the ballroom." I tried to write as fast as he spoke, but jotted down notes that could remind me.

"Okay, good...and in the ballroom, we need music. We will need some sort of violin or something at the very least for the people to dance to," I stated as I wrote 'music' on the list.

"I know a guy in town that will gladly come to host the evening's music. I will ask him for a price and let you guys know," George said. He was actually much more helpful than I thought he'd be. I gave him a quick smile before getting back to writing away. Part of me thought he wasn't all that terrible, but I still felt uneasy deep down.

"Let's make this a masquerade ball. How does that sound?" I asked, seeming to come up with the idea as I spoke. I only ever heard of these balls from stories I was told, and it had always been a dream of mine.

"Hmm...I guess we could do that," he said, seemingly uninterested.

"Another thing is the food. We need to tell James...I mean," I blurted out without thinking. I always associated him with being the chef of the kitchen.

"Wait, what did you say?" George asked, taking a serious tone all of a sudden.

"It's nothing, it's no one." I fidgeted to come up with an excuse of some sort, but was more surprised by his tone when I mentioned the name.

"How do you know of him?" He pushed further.

"I just heard a story of him, that's all…" I didn't want to tell him about my encounter with him and how Alice told me all about how he died.

"Be careful, Angeline…there are rumors here that one should not be so quick to believe," his face turned from grim back to a warm smile in the matter of seconds. It was a mask.

"What do you know of it?" I wanted to hear his side of the story.

"Not much. James worked for us and then he just took off and no one ever heard from him again, unfortunately. Some worker he was…" He shrugged and changed the subject back to the grand opening. I did not bring up James again after the suspicious response that he gave. How could the owner of a home not have any knowledge of a drowning? Unless, he would have been a suspect if one of his workers was found to have been drowned... I suddenly wanted nothing to do with the man that sat just a few inches away from me. I wanted to be far from this stranger who lied through his teeth to me. In the same moment I was about to flee the room and not look back, I decided to put the same mask on that he had all this time and smile back. Being in the same room as a man that could've been capable of one of the most animalistic ways of murder was one thing, but letting him know that I was fully aware of how James truly died was an advantage I could not let him have.

Calm

13

Days had passed, and I hadn't seen George around much, which heightened my suspicions even more. Aside from Alice and Mary, who were usually great company, I felt very alone. Father frequently went into town each day and even ended up purchasing the paddle boat from George and his family so that he would be able to leave much more easily. There were many times that I was tempted to wake up extra early so that I could take the paddle boat back to the mainland and somehow find Calian. Every morning, something caused me to back out. After one of Father's travels, he came home around noon with a paper rolled up and tied with a piece of string in the center.

"Who is this from?" I asked, as he handed it over to me.

"Your love, George, of course…" Father laughed at his joke and I immediately went on defense.

"I do not love him. He's just helping with the opening." I rolled my eyes and walked off with the scroll. His laughter continued until it eventually faded into silence and I found myself back in the living room space where I had originally planned the event with George. Upon sitting down, I creaked one of the windows open to let the cool afternoon breeze in. I had to flatten out the wrinkly letter several times against the edge of the table in order to read it. After pressing it down again and again, I decided to set the ink container on one corner and the feather pen on the diagonal one.

Lady Angeline,

It has been my pleasure to help you the other day with your upcoming ball. What a splendid idea it was to include music and dancing; I would surely love to attend this ball alongside you. I have been in touch with the musician and he has accepted the terms of employment for the night. Details of this arrangement shall be worked out accordingly. I will be coming back tomorrow at some point to meet with you and your father. We can discuss final plans since the event is just in two days!

Fondly,

George

What hint did I ever give off that I was interested? The way that he wrote it seemed like a letter from one lover to another. I clenched my jaw upon reading the last part and wished I could unread it. At least the music was all set for the night, but the food would have to be arranged. I glanced up toward the door and wondered if Alice and Mary were still in the kitchen despite it being just after lunch. I left the letter out on the table and drifted into the foyer then quickly rushed past the office so as not to have to deal with Father's remarks about my so called 'love' with George and was relieved when I saw Alice washing dishes in the sink. She still had the bonnet on that she commonly wore to keep her blonde hair out of the food and jumped upon my entering.

"How are you today, madam?" she asked, shaking off the sudden scare that I gave her. I instantly felt bad that she was stuck inside doing chores all the time while Father and I got to plan an event and enjoy the outdoors. I glanced over toward the picnic basket that was on the shelf and grabbed it.

"I was wondering if you wanted to come outside with me, we can bring some bread and maybe you can help me plan the food that will be available at the event?" I asked as I took a few pieces of bread and loaded the empty basket. Her eyes lit up right away.

"Oh, of course!" She seemed as surprised as I was. "Let me just finish up with these dishes and we can be on our way."

"Great, I'm so happy you can accompany me." I smiled at her and eyed the fruit that remained in the fruit bowl. Three lone apples. I shoved two of them in the basket and made a mental note that the last one could be a treat for Kitchi if I ever did see her again.

"I've never seen someone look so happy when looking at an apple," she noted, and I felt my cheeks heat in an instant.

"They are good! Alright, let's head out," I said as I took the picnic basket in one arm and interwove my other with hers. We were both cheerfully laughing when we passed Father who looked quite occupied in whatever paperwork was piled on his desk.

"Nice day for a picnic," he observed. We nodded and continued on through the front door. The calming breeze could've sent me into a lull, and it was just cloudy enough that the sun peeked out every so often. On the tree to the right was the blackbird that had an orange patch on its wing. I looked at it for a moment as we walked on, straying from the main path that I would normally take to the beach.

"That's a red-winged blackbird." Alice seemed to notice my intent gaze on it. "Each bird is unique in that they have a different patch of orange in various places. Some say that if you see one, it means you have guardians watching over you."

"Do you believe in that?" I asked, unsure of my own beliefs.

"Of course. There has got to be somewhere we go after our souls leave our bodies," she quickly assured me. It made sense, but for some reason, I couldn't seem to process the thought in my mind.

"I lost my mother several years ago and I always wonder where she is. I think about whether or not there is an afterlife all the time." I was surprised that I actually said this thought that frequented my mind aloud.

"Well, whatever kind of afterlife there is, be sure that her spirit lives on through the very fact that you are here." She was very wise...actually much more intelligent than any of the wealthy nobles I had met. It was quite alarming at the fact that someone could be so brilliant yet constrained by the norms of society to the point that they could only achieve so much.

"Thank you for that," I said as we found a clear grassy area just before the coastline of the island. Alice had brought a blanket, and I placed down the basket so that I could hold one side and help her spread it out on the ground. We had an open view of the mainland, and I was instantly glad that we chose the spot that we did.

"So, what kind of food are you looking to have present at this event?" she asked, getting onto the main purpose for our picnic.

"I'm not sure. It will be in the evening so that wouldn't be the main meal. It would just have to include some small plates," I said as I took out a piece of bread and handed it over to Alice. She had taken her bonnet off and her hair out of the bun, revealing long golden locks that went down to the middle of her back. The sun seemed to glimmer off each strand.

"How about some dumplings and tea available for anyone interested?" she suggested as she ripped the bread in half, munching on one of the pieces.

"That sounds simple enough. What about some fruits, too? In this area, we have apples, strawberries, and blueberries. We can make a tray of those to walk around with as the guests arrive and dance," I said, coming up with ideas as I talked on.

"Brilliant! And I can gather some tables from the closets, so people have a place to sit in the corners of the ballroom. It will be splendid!" She sounded more excited than I. Something caught my eye on the mainland, but I couldn't quite make it out.

"Hang on, I am going to walk to the shore real quick," I said as I left Alice behind. A deep longing grew in my core as I drew closer and closer to the waters. I rushed forward in an attempt to see more clearly and nearly walked right into the water in the process.

"Careful!" Alice pulled me back as I was about to soak my shoes. I hadn't noticed that she followed me. "What's out there?" she asked. I finally was able to squint hard enough to make out a small deer with a man close by. It had to be Calian.

"Promise you won't tell anyone?" I looked over at her, then at the absence of the pathway that would've led me to the mainland.

"The first day that I came here…before we even purchased the land, that man right there had warned me not to come." I looked down, then back up at her. "He told me of the history here and hauntings." She only nodded in response, and it made me want to explain even more. "Well, I had been seeing strange things that I cannot explain and the warnings about going out at night just don't make sense."

"You're right," she confirmed my thoughts. And here I was thinking that I had been crazy the whole time.

"I just can't seem to get him off my mind," I admitted.

"Let me tell you something…" She took my hand, and we walked back over to the blanket. "There was a time that I had a love and I was ignorant to follow my heart after him. Then one day, I found out that it was too late. I was forced to bury my emotions and go on with life as if nothing ever happened." A tear streamed down her cheek as she breathed in hard.

"What happened to him?" I asked, having a feeling that I knew who she was talking about.

"We were paid extra not to talk about how James drowned anymore to anyone at all. So I couldn't even mourn him properly," she began sobbing. I knelt beside her and held her in my arms, rubbing her back as I remembered mother would commonly do for me to calm me down.

"I had a feeling there was more to the story…" I said.

"I am not supposed to be telling you this," she admitted.

"Alice, what do you think happened to him?" I asked, trying to gain more information of the uncertain past of the island. She breathed in and exhaled, then squeezed her eyes shut a few times as to blink away the tears.

"I don't know, but all I know is that he didn't always get along with the owners here and then one day…he was just gone without explanation. I saw him walk into the waters to drown himself…but that's the thing. The James I knew would've never done that. I always felt like someone forced him." Her eyebrows furrowed, and she looked as though she wanted to get revenge against whoever killed her love. "All I am saying is, if you have a strong feeling in your heart, you need to chase and follow it."

Awakened

14

The quiet depths of night blanketed the air in an uneasy embrace. All seemed still except for the unending dance of the waves as they crept up the sandy shores and retreated out again and again. As I lay there in bed, I couldn't help but toss and turn at my conflicted thoughts. I felt as though I was drowning in expectations. So many unanswered questions filled my mind. From the very first day that we arrived, this island had been full of wonder — but, there were so many occurrences that couldn't simply be explained. Things that I had never seen happen on the mainland. I glanced over at my nightstand and picked up the cup that had been full of water. As I pressed it to my lips and cocked my head back, only the tiniest of drops entered my mouth. Part of me wished to just forget about my thirst and simply go back to sleep, but I knew I'd just continue to toss and turn if I ignored it.

There was just a sliver of light from the moon that let in through the window, but other than that, I stumbled to get to the nearest candle that wasn't lit. After several struggled attempts at lighting the candle, the dim flame flickered and I was on my way downstairs, careful not to wake anyone. I had never walked around at night in the house and although the quiet was peaceful, it was also unnerving and left me even more on edge. The kitchen was fully cleaned without a single dish in the sink. I set down the cup under the faucet and let water stream down. Just behind the sink was a window which showed the nearly full moon. I watched outside as there was just enough of a clearing between the trees to see out to the water. I wondered how Alice could've stayed here after all the tragedy that occurred. A few drops of rain trickled down from above, some hitting the window. As the air cooled outside, my presence on the other side caused the window to fog. Before I could wipe it away, I remembered the living room window I had left open. I scurried across the house, not remembering to tiptoe and, as I did so, the pouring rain crashed down. The floor beside the window already had a puddle, and I hurried to close it so that no more could be let in. Upon closing it, the same fog that had been in the kitchen window now spread across this one.

I walked over to set the candle down on the table and came back to the window, wiping it with my hand. The cool drops of condensation pressed into my palm. I slightly ducked and peered outside, curious. The trees were blowing wildly in the wind while the rain came down relentlessly. What once was a calm night turned into a storm that I hadn't seen in a very long time. It seemed to come from nowhere. As I continued to look out, I felt as though I was being watched.

An uncontrollable fear grew from deep within my core. I briefly glanced back and saw nothing but an empty room. When I looked back in the window as I had been all along, the figure of a man stood tall as a reflection In the foggy window that I had cleared once again. This time, I turned around to find the man just a few feet away from me. As soon as I caught his eye, the candlelight blew out, and I ran as fast as I could back up the stairs and toward my bedroom. As soon as I got there, the room was locked. I jiggled it repeatedly and found it was no use. For some reason, in all of my panic, no one seemed to hear me and wake up. I looked across the hall at Father's room and wondered if I should try that door, but before I could take a step forward to head there, the man began to walk up the steps and turned toward me on the other side of the hall. His eyes were dark and sullen, face lifeless. The apron that he wore was no longer the white that I had originally seen, but instead a dark brownish yellow. Seaweed draped over both of his shoulders and he looked completely soaked. If it weren't for the apron, I wouldn't have been able to guess that it was James. He just stared for a brief moment from across the hall as I questioned which way to turn. In the next instant, a mischievous smile crept upon his face as he lunged toward me. I desperately jiggled the doorknob again and fell forward as it opened from the inside. I heard the door slam behind me and wanted to just lie there on the floor and not look up. I wanted the ground to open up and take me — take me away from this horror. I felt a warm hand touch my wrist; much different from what I would expect from a ghost who had just been in the water. But who had been in my room?

"Please, leave me alone!!" I started sobbing into the floor, afraid to look up. Afraid of what I would have to face; I would rather be blind to whatever was waiting for me to turn around. They touched my arm again and began to rub my back.

"Get your hands off me!" I said and at this point, turned, not caring of the outcome as everything had been leading up to my sure demise. A man that was pretty much the opposite of James was kneeling beside me as he gently grasped both of my wrists and stared into my eyes.

"You're okay now. Take deep breaths," Calian assured me. My once sunken heart now lifted in hope.

"How did you get—" I began to ask, but choked on my own words as the tears poured down my cheeks, matching the sky outside. He pulled me in close for a hug and rubbed my back in smooth circles.

"In...and out..." he whispered as I tried to think of those three words as I breathed. Being able to focus on that seemed to help, but did not even begin to crack the surface of agitation that I felt. As I pressed my head against his bare chest, I felt a warmth that breathed hope back into me. A warmth that had been taken away so quickly just before. He became a refuge for me even in the darkest of nights.

"When I warned you not to come here, I had a feeling you wouldn't listen," he said. "So when it is close to the full moon, the worst of the curse comes." When I looked outside, it appeared as though we would have our full moon sometime over the next two days. That would mean on the grand opening night, the curse would be at its highest potential.

"Did you see him?" I asked, putting all of my other questions on hold. I still held on to him and refused to fully leave his side. Where I had just pressed my cheek up against his chest, I now looked right into his eyes, heart still racing a mile a minute. He nodded in response.

"I know what it looks like, but I felt a great need to protect you tonight — something told me to come and wait in here, just in case. I snuck in when no one was looking," he explained his presence in my bedroom. I felt my eyebrows furrow in anger, but they softened when I quickly remembered how he had saved me and if it weren't for him, who knew what would have come of me?

"What was he doing here? How did he get in?" I asked, walking away to sit on the side of my bed. He remained kneeling where he was and looked my way, radiating even from just the sliver of moonlight.

"The evil spirits lurk outside and your house has been blessed time and time again with holy water so that they cannot enter…but…sometimes they can find openings," he explained. I put my head down in my hands, aggravated with myself.

"The window…the window downstairs. I left it open from yesterday," I sighed. He seemed to feel my frustrations as he walked over and touched my shoulder. "How can we keep everybody safe on the night of the event?" My mouth kept spewing out questions as the worries flooded my mind.

"You make sure to keep the visitors inside, but whoever leaves must depart before sunset. It's summer, so the sun should set much later in the evening," he reassured me.

"I don't know how I'm going to do this." I laid back on the bed in defeat. A wave of exhaustion overcame me as I struggled to keep my eyes open.

"Please...stay," I requested as his soft, chestnut brown eyes became cloudy, then blurred, and finally all I saw was nothingness.

Warning

15

A symphony of birds filled my ears as I clung to an extra pillow, hugging it as I would another person. At first, I had thought it was someone else but was quick to realize it wasn't when I hugged tighter and it gave no response. I reluctantly opened my eyes just to quickly close them again due to the intense light beaming in through the windows. I pulled the covers over my head and wished for a darker blanket to seal the light away. In my efforts to hide, I peeked back out at the window from across the room and remembered. Surveying the room from wall to wall, there was no sign of him. I leapt out of bed and pressed my body flat to the floor beside it to check underneath. Nothing. I walked over to the vanity and looked in the mirror, finding that I had dark bags under my eyes and my hair was disheveled, as if I went through a tornado. It took a second, but I decided how I would spend my day and wobbled back over to bed, legs feeling like they'd collapse from underneath me at any moment. The bed sheet wasn't thick enough to block out all light, but turning my face into the pillow should do the job.

"And what are you doing, little miss?" I had thought at least Alice would possibly walk in, but not her mother... I groaned. "You know, George is already downstairs waiting on you."

Even more reason not to get out of bed.

I heard Mary as she opened up the doors to my wardrobe and rummaged through various dresses to pick out my outfit for the day. She must have thought of me as a child...a helpless child. At this point, that is exactly how I felt. Especially after last night. I had to get through the meeting with George so that I could at least come up with a plan with Alice...and hopefully find Calian. He seemed to know far more than I did and could be of great help. I decided to give in and got up, heading over to the wardrobe as Mary handed me the dress. I didn't really mind what I was going to wear that day.

"Did you hear the storm last night?" I asked, walking behind the changing wall and shimmying into the beige dress.

"Storm?" she asked, surprised. "You must have been dreaming." She quickly brushed the thought off, and I stood behind the wall, puzzled. I would have to talk to Alice. She had said that all the staff were paid not to say much, and I was sure that Alice was opening up more whereas Mary was not likely to as much.

"I guess so," I agreed, half-heartedly. "He's already here?" I asked of George. She nodded and began combing my hair as I applied makeup in front of the vanity. Within the drawers, I pulled out the opal earrings and put one in each ear, followed by the pendant I draped around my neck as Mary clasped the back. This was the one piece of jewelry I frequented because it matched with pretty much everything.

"You know, when I was a young girl like you — I would have fallen head over heels for a man like

George." She went on about his financial status and how he could support a family... I felt a tug on each side of my head and realized that she was pulling half of my hair into a bun while leaving the rest down. This would be a new one.

"I just don't like him. Something seems off about him." I could at least say that much to her.

"What is it about him that you don't like?" She pressed to know more.

"I can't really explain it." I got up from sitting at the vanity and turned to Mary. "Thank you for helping me. What you did with my hair looks beautiful." She smiled and I could tell she likely missed the days of doing her own daughter's hair.

"I never liked him much either," she admitted, which was odd because it counteracted her initial suggestion of going after him.

"Hey, where's Alice?" She was usually the one to help me each morning.

"Oh, uh…she has been feeling under the weather of late, so she is resting. I hope that's okay with you." Mary looked down at her feet as if she was concealing something.

"Of course that's ok. Are you sure she's alright?" I asked, hoping she would tell me more.

"Oh yeah, she will be alright," she said. There was nothing more that I could say, as it seemed she was pretty closed off to the idea. Before heading out of the bedroom, I breathed in deeply and closed my eyes to have one last break from putting the mask on my face yet again, concealing my true feelings from the world. The storm that had once encompassed the skies around was now gone and out of sight; a distant memory that seemed to just be my own. Strokes of sunlight beamed in through the windows and reflected onto the foyer's wooden floors, causing them to shine. George was waiting at the door, his dirty blonde hair slicked back and parted a few inches above his right ear. A clean-shaven face as per usual and light blue eyes that softened his face. Surprisingly, a dark frock coat draped over his arm, as it was far too hot for him to bring it in the first place. But who was I to judge? The rest of his ensemble was relatively plain, being that he had trousers that went up to his waist-line and a loosely cut button-down shirt.

"Lady Angeline. My, you look gorgeous today," he exclaimed. My beige dome-shaped skirt made my waist appear even smaller than it was and above, I had a white blouse that normally hid underneath a day jacket, but due to the summer, it was unnecessary.

"Thank you." I gave him a quick smile, and he took my hand when I reached the last step, helping me to get to the floor. I wasn't going to forget of the worries that constantly swarmed my mind. I will admit that he looked quite pleasant today… "You are looking fine as well."

"Okay, you two, our big event is tomorrow night, so we are going to need everything in order. Go on and make a checklist for the day," Father suggested as his head was stuck in a book and he wandered off into the office again. What he did in there, only God knew.

George and I just looked at one another and my thoughts jumped to Alice. Something in me told me to check on her. It was very unlike her to just not show up and she had been fine just yesterday.

"I will be right down, let's meet out back ok?" I requested, trying to buy myself some more time to go check on Alice as I headed back upstairs. George had a puzzled look on his face upon my leaving, but headed outside anyway. I wouldn't have been able to focus on anything if I didn't at least check on Alice. She lived in one of the smaller rooms with her mother, and it was in the farthest corner of the second floor.

I gave a gentle knock, and there was no response. Each time, I made sure to be a little louder so that she would hear better if she was actually even in there.

"Alice, are you okay?" I called from the other side of the door. There was still no response. I jiggled the doorknob to find that it was unlocked and opened it to see that Alice was still in the bed, facing away from the door. I rushed over to the other side of the bed so that I could see her face. Her eye was swollen and bruised up with patterns of purple and deep red. Above her eyebrow was a cut that looked fairly recent and she lay in the fetal position in bed, hugging the pillow as I had the night before. I touched her shoulder, at which point she winced.

"What happened to you?!" I exclaimed, carefully taking my hand off the shoulder that clearly hurt. She just groaned and turned her head more into the pillow. "Come on, Alice. Talk to me. Who did this to you?"

"I can't—" she grunted out.

"Can't what?!" I pleaded

"Say."

"Come on, you know you can tell me anything," I said. "I won't tell anyone and I can help!" I assured her as I held my hand out to try to help her sit up in bed. I felt her delicate hand touch mine as she laid all her weight onto me and I gently lifted her up so she could sit against the back bedpost. She slowly opened her right eye, that was still swollen.

"You shouldn't be here. I'll get in more trouble," she said.

"In trouble by who?" I asked. Father and I owned this house, so there was no reason for her to face any consequences, especially when she hadn't done anything wrong in the first place.

"Him..." she said, gulping down hard. In the next second, a man called from downstairs.

"Coming, Angeline?! I've been waiting outside," George hollered from downstairs. At the mere sound of his voice, Alice winced and began to grab her pillow as if to shield herself.

"George?" I quickly asked.

"Please go quick before he comes. Don't tell him you saw me," she desperately urged. "He found out that I told you about James..." I felt my jaws clench in fury. Alice had said that George's family paid the staff extra to stay hushed about what had happened. And she told me, but it wasn't really her. It was that night that I saw James. Or I thought I saw him... In any case, if he was willing to do this to poor, defenseless Alice...then there was no knowing what else he was capable of.

Mask

16

"Coming!" I shouted. I abruptly jumped up and ran out of Alice's room before he found that I was there. I heard him as he ascended up the steps, but was just walking past Father's room when I was in visible sight of him.

"What were you doing?" he asked.

It took everything in my power to walk toward the animal that he was. At first, I questioned my lack of evidence…but at this point, I now had living proof that he was not truly who he said he was. But I had to go along with what he said. I couldn't let him in on all I knew, so that I could at least stay a step ahead of him and have some sort of advantage.

"Oh, uhm, I forgot I left the window open," I couldn't seem to come up with any other excuse.

He held out his hand and I could tell he didn't believe me, but we both wore our masks for one another, concealing all we truly knew. When I came up to him, I debated not holding his hand, but knew it would give me away for sure. I reluctantly took it and turned my head to the side, wincing from the very touch of this monster.

"So, out back, you said?" he asked. Being in the house a moment longer would've been pure suffocation for me in an instant.

"That sounds fine." I glanced back at him. As we went through the front door, he called over to the other maid.

"Mary, fetch us a blanket please and maybe a basket," he ordered, acting as if Mary was nothing but a dog — living to obey every demand without question. A few seconds later, she came with a basket in one hand and the blanket draped over the other. It had been the same blanket that Alice and I used just yesterday.

"Anything else you may need?" she nervously asked, ignoring my presence completely. Things were very strange, being that it seemed as though she was still working for him.

"No, that will do." He smiled and continued out the door beside me, handing me the picnic basket to carry as he held the blanket. Outside would have been a breath of fresh air if not for the unwanted company. We headed straight ahead instead of out back, as I had originally asked. We got all the way to the sandy shores, and he set down the blanket as I put the basket in the middle, not bothering to open it.

"What's the matter?" He asked, and it caused me to jump out of my skin.

"Me? Oh, nothing," I answered, debating on reaching in the basket for some bread so that I could at least keep my hands busy.

"Are you sure? Ever since you came back downstairs it looked as though something scared you," he persisted on asking. "I don't bite." His last statement was ironic in itself.

"Yeah, yeah…I'm fine. So, let's talk about the event tomorrow night," I said, eager to change the topic so that we could get this picnic done and over with.

"The musician is all set. We have the food taken care of being that you spoke with Alice…" At the mention of her name, we both seemed to cringe, it seemed for different reasons entirely. "Now… all that is left is to make the raffle cards so people can fill their name out and place it into a bowl of some sort so you can draw from there."

"Good idea, we should get back so I can go finish all of that up." I got up, only to be pulled back by his grasp around my wrist. Despite the scorching sun beaming directly onto us, his light blue eyes sent a cold chill down my spine.

"Stay a while, we haven't finished talking," he said as I sat back down.

"What else is there to talk about?" I asked, curious.

"Us." His body drew closer to mine so that he was leaning in and I turned my head in such a way that he ended up planting his lips on my cheek. "Oh, don't be shy." I felt his hand grip my chin as he turned my head and pressed his lips into mine. My heart sank to the bottom of my chest as an anchor would, holding its whole crew back for some time. Instead, with this anchor...I felt as though the entirety of my being was sinking...drowning...I jumped up right away, too quick for him to grab and pull me down again.

"I think you have me misunderstood." I tried to be as polite as I could when all I felt like doing was screaming for help.

"If little Alice ruined this for us…I am going to have to talk with her again," he warned. Flashes of Alice's bruised up face rushed through my mind and I didn't want to know what else would happen if George didn't get his way. I turned and faced the calm of the waves, wishing they, too, could just take me away with them. As the tide receded and the path revealed more and more, I wished to go down that path back to the mainland. I needed to get to Calian. He would know what to do. I thought of my mom and the lessons that she had left me with throughout the short time I had her in my life. One distinct lesson was to protect those that we love…even if it meant we would suffer for a bit. Protect those that are dear to us as we would want the same protection in return. But even if there was no return, we could still go to bed at the end of the day knowing we at least tried. In that moment, I decided I would wear that mask if it meant protecting my friend. I would have to pretend all was okay and it would be one of the hardest things I had done my whole life. I turned around and smiled at George as he packed up a few things.

"How would Alice ruin anything? I just don't want to rush things." I pretended to be dumbfounded at the very idea he had. As I walked toward him, he seemed to be stumped and no words left his mouth. "We are going to see one another at the ball, no?" I asked.

"Yes...I mean...well, of course," he stammered.

"Well then, I look forward to seeing you then, George," I lied through my teeth.

"So you'll be my date?" he asked, and I knew it was all a game to him. A game in which he wanted to win a prize, and that prize was me. But once he won…once he thought he won, I would be trapped with this monster for life. I couldn't let him win the game, but I at least intended on buying more time until the grand opening was done and over with.

"I look forward to it," I mimicked my earlier response. "Now, let me get back inside so that we can make this happen."

"You are a woman after my own heart." He bit his lip as if to hold back a sudden urge to grasp my arm again and pull me in towards him. I buried my feelings of resentment and hurt, nodding his way as I sealed the lie with a smile.

17

George seemed to believe every word I said once I pretended to be interested in him. He walked me up the front steps of the inn and set off, as he had other business to attend. At first, I was going to check on Alice, but instead stared through the side of the window and watched the monster as he left the island. He jumped in his paddle boat which was right beside the pathway that now fully extended toward the mainland, making it perfectly walkable. As he drew further away from the shore, he became smaller and smaller until I could barely see him any longer.

"What are you looking at?" Father asked, causing me to jump. He walked beside me and kissed my forehead. "Geez, you're as frightened as a mouse!"

"I'm ok, Father," I said. "I may go for a walk, if that's okay?"

"Oh yeah, sure thing! Want me to come with you?" he suggested. Any other time, I would've gladly accepted his offer. But this time, I had to do it on my own. If I involved Father in the mess I found, it would only get worse. It was better off to go on happy in life and be blind to some of the evil things in this world as opposed to knowing all the bad and leading a miserable life. And he deserved to be happy, at the very least.

"No, that's okay, maybe after the grand opening. How's that?" I asked.

"Well, don't go far." He gave me a strong hug to the point that I felt squished.

"Too tight, hey," I said, jokingly

"What? You want an even bigger hug?" he joked, but I knew what would come next. He picked me up and hugged me even tighter as my legs dangled in the air. I could feel my cheeks turn bright red.

"Alright, alright, put me down," I said after he had his enjoyment. Father just laughed, and it made my heart feel less sunken just by hearing his happiness.

"Don't go too far, ok?" His sausage fingers wrapped around the doorknob as he pulled it open to let me out.

"I won't. I love you!"

"I love you a hundred!" he shouted as I walked down the steps of the front porch. This was a game we had because when I was younger, I had thought a hundred was the highest possible number. So when I would tell him that I loved him, it was always a hundred. Whoever got the last word in won.

"No, no, no, 200!" I joked, knowing full well now that a hundred was definitely not the highest number.

"Impossible. That doesn't exist!" he called out and closed the door, showing he had won that game. As I continued on down the path that led to the sandy pathway, I felt a brief moment of peace in that I still had love in my heart. And for as long as I still felt that, I knew there was still hope.

Waves sloshed back and forth against the path that formed with low tide. I had a straight shot down to the mainland, but wasn't quite sure when it would no longer be present. The further I walked, the longer the path became, and I wasn't even sure if I would see Calian or at least be able to find him. I was on a mission without a plan and blindly walking to the mainland alone, not knowing how I would be able to get back. But I still continued on, despite all the uncertainty that lay before me. The only sound that filled the air aside from the constant waves were from the seagulls soaring above. Any shells that washed up with the tide, they would take up high with them and drop them so that they would crack open, at which point they would devour the creature inside.

As I thought about the fact that my time was running out for the pathway, I began walking faster and faster. I could feel my shoes sink in the wet sand but continued on, ignoring it along with the pain it caused me. The only shoes I had in my wardrobe were mainly for dressing up and they did not suit walking around a lot. On and on I went, the house and island behind me appearing smaller by the minute. When I finally reached the shores of the mainland, I saw the paddle boat that had been pulled up on the sand far above where high tide would go. It was also tied around a giant rock by a rope. That could be my Plan B if the tides washed up the pathway that led back to the island. It was a relief to be back on the mainland and away from the island. I looked back out at it and although small in size, I felt less trapped, at least being off of it, although it still had a bit of a hold on me.

As I turned around, I slowly walked over to the bush where Kitchi had been and Calian slowly stroking her side. I distinctly remembered that night he saved me and my last request was just for him to stay by my side...but he seemed to have vanished in the night somehow and was no longer there. I didn't understand why he didn't stay, but perhaps that was my own greed getting in the way. If we had spent hours together, it would have surely felt like mere minutes flashing by. No amount of time would have been good enough and here I was on the mainland seeking this man who I felt as safe around as my own father, despite him being a complete stranger. I wished I had brought an apple to possibly lure Kitchi back, but it was too late. I decided to walk the coastline, no longer fearing being unable to travel back due to the boat being there. Father hated being out in the sun, but I wished he was walking beside me so I could at least have some company and we could make jokes at one another. As the waters rose, I decided to take my shoes off and carried my skirt up a bit as not to get it wet. I purposely stepped closer to the edge of the shores to feel the cool water on my toes. I giggled as the salt tickled between my toes. The refreshing ocean drifted over the entirety of my feet and then retreated back again.

"Are you having fun over there?" A familiar voice called out. I felt butterflies in my stomach and turned to find Calian standing just a few feet away, emerging from the bushes that separated the forest of trees and sand. His sun-kissed skin glimmered and looked almost mystical, as if he were a being from another world. His long, black hair was perfectly straight and blew in the wind, much different from my wavy, dark hair. I wanted to run my fingers through it.

"Oh yes, of course…" I said as I dipped my toes in the water again and winced at the shocking cold that overcame me from doing so. He just chuckled.

"Where's Kitchi?" I asked, looking out to see that his little friend was nowhere around.

"Oh, she's resting. Some creature must have attacked her and my tribe has been treating her wounds." He looked down.

"Is she going to be ok?" I asked, noticing how similar our lives now were. His friend, Kitchi and also my friend, Alice, were both resting from being attacked. It reminded me of my purpose for the endeavor to set out for the mainland in the first place.

"Yes, she'll be ok. Caught her just in time." He began walking toward me and came as close to the water as I was, also dipping his bare feet in. Unlike me, he didn't wince in the slightest at the cold as it spread over his toes.

"Why did you leave?" I wanted to know why I had to wake up to an empty room on such a night of horror.

"I stayed the whole night, but left in the morning." His body was turned away from me as he stared out at the island.

"Oh." I felt embarrassed at my accusation.

"The next full moon will be tomorrow night and that is when your grand opening is."

"It's George. George is the evil presence on the island," I blurted out, and he faced me right away.

"I had a feeling…"

"But how could he be if he is still alive? His spirit cannot lurk on the island…" I was hoping he could explain this part that I worked through in my mind again and again, but still couldn't reach an understanding.

"You see…" He took my hand in his and grasped it gently. My hand nearly disappeared in his, as it was so much bigger in comparison. "There are good and bad spirits — both living and dead. Sometimes, we fear the dead because we cannot see them and we are uncertain about what happens in death. But there are great evils in this world that live within people.

"My tribe has watched over the island from afar and made sure to warn travelers," he continued. "But we have always been too late."

"What does this mean of George, though?" Calian let go of my hand and looked back out at the island.

"While we have watched over the land, we've seen and heard many strange things…and many of those things were when George's family bought the island. At first, there were several people that they hired. One by one, we saw less of them..." he admitted.

"So, you mean to say that it is possible that George killed them?" I asked, wanting to mention the state of which I found Alice this morning.

"It is possible, Angeline..." My name sounded like velvet coming from his lips.

"I'm scared." I looked over at him, taking in every inch of his arms — muscular and warm. I instantly wanted them around me. I felt his hand on my shoulder and goosebumps lined my arms at his touch. "What if someone comes in again tonight?"

"I'll be there," he promised.

Concealed

18

Calian agreed to come at the next low tide and we separated as not to be found by anyone. The pathway was halfway concealed by the time I got back to the start of it. I thanked the heavens for the paddle boat. Upon getting in, it felt like it took forever to paddle all the way back to the island. Every time I thought I was nearing the coastline of the island, the waves seemed to just push me back out to undo the effort I had just put in. I thought of George putting his hands on Alice and it enraged me. I wished I was there to help stand up for her, as she must have been so afraid and alone. It was a wonder how long it had been going on for… and they couldn't even stand up for themselves because they were of lower social status than he. No one would have believed any of the staff and they could barely escape the island to begin with. When I got back, I'd ask Alice if she wanted to go for a walk with me to the mainland so that she could at least feel free again. It's what I would've wanted done for me if I was in the same position.

As I became closer, I realized Father was standing at the entry of the path that was now just about washed up completely. He had both of his hands on his sides and looked very displeased. Part of me wanted to turn the boat around and go the other way, but I knew I would have to face him sooner or later. He saw me struggling to get out of the boat upon reaching the sandy shores and held out his hand in an attempt to help despite his clear frustration in me.

"Don't go far…what would far mean to you, then?" He asked, shaking his head.

"Well…uhm…" I bit my lip as we both dragged the boat farther onto the land and he took the rope to tie it around a nearby rock so that it wouldn't go anywhere.

"What do I have to do, Ange? It's not safe out there alone," he said, but didn't know the half of it. I was at least safer out there than on this distorted island… "Where has your mind gone?" He snapped me out of my thoughts.

"I don't know, Father...I'm sorry." I didn't know what else to say. We walked back toward the inn and when we reached the steps, he stopped right in front of me, eyes looking tearful.

"You're all I've got, Ange. What if something happened to you? I don't know what I would do," he admitted and looked down as if to conceal that he was crying.

"Nothing is going to happen to me. I'm here, I'm here," I said and hugged him, not getting anywhere close to reaching my arms fully around him. He pressed his head into my shoulder and I felt the tears seep into my dress. I instantly felt guilty for making him worry and feel this way. I wanted to tell him everything, but didn't know if or how he would understand.

"I have to tell you something," I started. He looked up as he wiped his tears.

"I do not think George is good," I continued, since his silence seemed to tell me to keep going. "I found that the staff had been tortured by him." At once, his eyebrows furrowed, and he picked up my arms, inspecting them.

"Has he laid his hands on you?! I swear... I will..."

"No, no, he hasn't! I'm okay! It's just the staff and from when his family owned this island. I think he is bad news," I said, worried that he wouldn't believe me. I wasn't even going to begin talking about the paranormal that I had seen.

"Well, we mustn't allow his presence back here," he decided.

"We can't do that. We can't let him know or I think bad things will happen," I said, wishing I hadn't brought it up.

"Angeline. I am not letting a man that abuses women anywhere near you, let alone in the place that we reside." He was not going to back down and started up the steps to go into the house. Just before he was about to enter, I pulled on his arm.

"His family...his family is wealthy and very powerful. We cannot do this or we will suffer the consequences." I tried to make him face the harsh reality of the world. It was true.

"He comes to the grand opening...and then we never see his smug face again," he warned, and I felt my heart stop for a brief moment. I had no idea what would happen when Father laid eyes on George, but it wasn't going to be good. I would continue to wear the mask that I had so carefully built as not to give away anything to him. When we walked in, Father followed me up to the maids' room so that I could show him what George did to Alice. I knocked and this time, we heard a response.

"Come in!" She sounded much more delightful than before, which was strange because it had just been this morning that she was on the brink of a coma, it seemed. Father and I exchanged a glance at one another and both entered. Alice had her bonnet on and not a single strand of her blonde hair hung down as it was carefully tied back. She was fully dressed and walking around the room, straightening up.

"Are you doing better?" I asked, confused as to the sudden shift.

"Never been better." She turned and showed the same face that I had seen yesterday, clear of any bruising whatsoever. It was as if nothing ever happened at all.

"What happened to your…?" I was lost.

"My what?" she said.

"Alice, you don't have to pretend. This morning, your face was completely bruised and now… you're fine. Father knows."

I hoped that would allow her to open up a little bit.

"I'm fine, just a little under the weather this morning," she insisted.

"Okay girls, I'm going to head downstairs. Believe it or not, we have a lot of planning to do for tomorrow night's opening," Father excused himself. I knew that he still had it out for George even though Alice showed no sign of having been beaten, but I wished Father was able to see what I saw. When he left us alone, I scurried over to Alice to find out what was going on.

"Alice, I saw you this morning and your face was all bruised from George. I saw you and you looked near death. And now, you are suddenly fine without a bruise to convey what happened?" I wanted answers, but only seemed to get more questions.

"Oh...you worry too much! I'm okay, actually I've never been better," she lied through her teeth. She and I both knew it.

"Alice, we are going to make sure that George doesn't come back here again. We'll see that he is gone after the grand opening and you guys don't have to worry about him anymore," I promised. There was a slight quiver in her lip every time I mentioned his name.

She just kept walking around this way and that, ignoring what I said.

"Want some tea?" She began to head out of the room. It frustrated me even more.

"No, I'm fine. Okay, you may not want to talk about it right now...but whenever you are ready, I'm here," I confirmed the obvious of which I was sure she wasn't going to bring it up again to me. It seemed that she just wanted to forget about it and somehow... someway... concealed the evidence. Perhaps with some powder? It was too perfectly hidden.

The Truth

19

The remainder of the day dragged on, and I had made all the raffles papers for people to fill out. I even found a little table to set it on in the front once everyone entered. I figured this would add to the excitement. After that was done, I walked over to the shores because it was escape enough from being in the house. Nothing made sense anymore. As I peered out, I could see that the sun was just beginning to set and low tide would be coming shortly. I worried for Calian venturing out here during nightfall and was unsure if he would even make it. I wished I had told him not to come. He would be putting himself in danger just to protect me, which wasn't very wise… I decided to take the journal out of the satchel I wore and begin writing before the sun would set at least.

August 19, 1849

It is times like these that I want Mother most. I am scared of what's to come. I wish we had never moved here and part of me wants to sleep during the day so that I can stay awake each night just in case. I feel uneasy about closing my eyes here. I want to be on the mainland with Calian. I want to tell Father about him and hope that he approves. It is doubtful, but maybe if he sees me happy, he will be okay with it. There are so many strange things happening that I can't even think straight and what is even worse is that I have to face George tomorrow night and be his date for the entire evening.

Until next time,

Angeline

"Hey there you are." Alice came at just the right time when I had been putting the journal back into my satchel. "I just want to apologize about before."

"Why wouldn't you tell the truth?" I asked, moving over on the rock so that she had room to sit beside me.

"I just swept it under the rug because it is not something we need to worry about any longer," she said.

"How?"

"He is no longer a danger to us, and it's important that you just stay away from him. Okay?" She sincerely looked over at me like a lost little puppy that was looking for its home.

"I don't understand…but I had promised to be his date for tomorrow night's event," I revealed.

"Why would you do a thing like that?!" She jumped up from the rock and stood in front of me as if the words I said shocked her out of a daze.

"I thought he would hurt you more if I refused…or even come after my father. I made the decision in the matter of seconds." I frowned and looked down at my dress, rubbing my hand against the side so as to occupy myself with something.

"What about the man on the mainland? Calian?" She remembered his name surprisingly.

"Shhh, I want to keep that secret." She chuckled and sat beside me again.

"What did I say about going after your loved one?! I don't recall saying anything about agreeing to go to an event with someone else entirely and keeping your lover a secret!" Although she whispered, it still seemed like she was yelling, as her tone sounded angry with me. Almost as angry with myself as I was.

"I know, I know… looking back, I'm not sure what I was thinking. I didn't really care about my own wants. Instead, I was trying to just protect everyone else," I admitted.

"Okay…" She breathed in deeply and exhaled, then turned to me with a stern look on her face. "I am going to tell you something my mother once told me when I was young."

"Alright." I was all ears, aside from being quite distracted by my own thoughts.

"Each person is like a flower. If that flower just keeps giving its pollen away to help the bees, butterflies and everyone else but never gets watered, then it will eventually wither up and die. All those that the flower cared for will no longer have the support from which the flower used to give them, because it will be dead."

"I am the flower," I stated.

Alice nodded and waited for me to process what she had just said.

"The bees and butterflies are my family and friends, and I sacrifice myself in an effort to help them. But one day, I will have nothing left of my soul at the very least, as it will have been sacrificed fully." It all made sense.

"Exactly! When's the next time that you will see Calian?" she asked. Talking about him seemed to give me more purpose in life and excitement. It was the light in all this darkness that had become my life. I felt embarrassed to answer her question, so I just bit my lip and looked away.

"Come on...tell me!" she urged on.

"Tonight," I blurted out and continued avoiding eye contact with her.

"Oh my goodness!" she screamed and jumped up again as she had before, except this time with much more excitement. Alice grabbed both of my hands and started hopping up and down as if she was a little kid and had found a giant piece of chocolate.

"We're not doing anything, Alice!" I tried to brush off any thoughts that her mind likely wandered to.

"Still! Why tonight?" she asked, regaining her composure, but remained standing as she looked down at me. She let go of my hands.

"It's not safe at night here and I've been haunted. I just didn't want to be alone another night," I revealed and got up to walk back toward the house.

"Well, when is he coming?" She seemed to ignore what I had said about being scared.

"Shh, shh. Don't tell anyone! Low tide," I answered in a much more hushed tone as we approached the house.

"Oh, I am so excited for you. I've got to meet this man someday. Promise that?" she asked. I nodded, and we headed in, passing Father along the way toward the kitchen. My stomach gargled in hunger and I hadn't realized that I forgot to eat most of the day.

"You two look happy," Father noted as we walked by.

"We just went for a stroll. You'll have to come next time, sir," Alice covered for me, as I seemed terrible at coming up with excuses, although what she said was partly true. He didn't have to know what we had talked about.

"Alright girls, come here." He stopped us in our tracks. "I don't know what did or didn't happen, but even the slight accusation of someone putting their hands on someone else gets me flustered. So…" he said as he came out from the office and met us in the foyer.

"So?" I asked, kind of glad that he brought it back up.

"Angeline is right that their family can destroy us by the measure of their power and wealth. So tomorrow night will go as planned, but there will be no more mention of his name after that. You hear me?" he asked.

I still wasn't sure how he planned on keeping him away, but we both nodded our heads as if he was a drill sergeant and we were both reporting for duty.

"Go off and enjoy the rest of the day, for at least we still have our sanity for now," he murmured, heading upstairs to his room. Alice and I went the opposite way and continued on toward the back of the house. As we entered the ballroom, I showed her the raffle jar I made along with everything else. After going over all the details of the next day's festivities, we called it a day. Alice said that she was going to straighten up the kitchen, then head to bed, and when I found myself in the foyer, I couldn't help but peek out the window — hoping to already see Calian. But there was no sign of him. The darkened sky left me feeling hopeless. I trudged upstairs reluctantly and headed to bed, as that was the only thing there was left to do.

The Sign

20

I laid in bed for what felt like hours, unable to sleep. My mind kept flashing to horrifying thoughts of what could've possibly stopped Calian from being able to come back. Since my room was on the second floor of the house and faced the front, I mustered up the strength to at least look out the window. As I walked across the room, sudden fears of all of my surroundings made it even more difficult not to run back into bed and hide under the covers. I had to at least see if he was around, though. Maybe he couldn't get in. Maybe it was locked. But how was he able to get into the house the other night?

Outside, the night appeared calmer than it felt. The trees slightly blew with the breeze. It was almost inviting to go out there, even just to get a breath of fresh air. Past the trees was the pathway to its full extent at low tide. I squinted to try to see more clearly, but saw a speck that appeared to be moving closer along that same path. As it drew closer, I could tell it was a man hurrying toward the island. As the moonlight shone down on the waters, it slightly illuminated him to the point that I could tell it was Calian by his long hair.

As much as I felt like it was the best thing to wait indoors, I decided to get downstairs so I could let him in as soon as possible so he didn't get hurt by anything that lurked within the night. I left no windows open, so whatever had been let in the other night was bound to be trapped outside, unable to come in. As I neared the front door, I first peered out the window to see when Calian was close as I planned to open the door upon him reaching the front porch. I found him as he ran and edged closer and closer to the door. When he got there, we locked eyes as he saw me through the window. I gave him a smile and was just glad that he was able to make it. Giving the doorknob a quick turn, it barely moved. Locked. I tried again. No. It was happening again. But he was right there! I struggled with it repeatedly, and it wouldn't budge. The only way the door locked was from the inside; so I wasn't sure why it was stuck. As I walked back over to the window beside the door, I looked at him and shook my head, then remembered the exit out back and held up a finger as if to tell him to hold on one minute.

Rushing through the foyer and past the stairs that led up, I continued on until I reached the ballroom. The back door opened easily, and I ran out, making sure to close it behind me. I went around the side of the house that I hadn't gone through before. It wasn't cleared out as much and felt as though I was going through a forest as there was a plethora of trees. The nearly full moon was the only light that guided me through its darkness. I stumbled over a rock and fell to the ground in my rush to get to the front of the house. I could feel the dirt under my fingernails as I tried to pick myself back up. The bottom of my nightgown turned a deep red on the right side. I lifted it to find a cut on my ankle that I must've gotten from the rock. I winced in pain and tried to think of what I could use to stop the stream of blood as it left my body. There was nothing. To the right of me were bushes that seemed to hide a sliver of gray behind them. Limping over, I pushed part of one of the bushes to the side to find a tombstone. It looked as though it was engraved a long time ago.

Here Lies James Walton

May His Soul Rest In Peace

I stumbled back, careful not to fall again, disturbed by the hidden marker of his death. A cloud overhead moved past the moon, allowing it to beam down on two other tombstones that lay beside James'.

Mary Atwater

Beloved Mother, Rest In Peace

My mind went right to the maid, Mary. But that was a common name. One of the most common, in fact. I walk quick to calm myself down with that explanation but looked at the last tomb beside it that appeared much more recent as there was no grass over the mud before the stone.

Alice Atwater

Beloved Daughter, Rest In Peace

I felt my heart sink in my chest and instantly forgot about the wound that pained me to my core. I needed to get out of this graveyard before there was a tomb for my name next. Alice. Mary. It would've been too coincidental. There was no other explanation for both of their names on the tombstones. Mary was Alice's mother. They were both the maids at the house. And I had just seen Alice just a few hours ago. All I knew now was to run and keep running until I was safe, in his arms again. I reached the front porch and Calian was still there, peering into the window. He seemed to hear my gasping breaths as I limped up the steps and ran to my side, embracing his arms around my body.

"What happened?" he asked, concerned.

"I don't…I can't. Oh Calian, please help me!" I began sobbing uncontrollably. I didn't know where to start first and just wanted to leave and go some place far from here.

"It's ok, shh, I'm here now. Let's get you inside." He scooped me up as if I was as light as a feather to him. "Where can we enter?"

"Around…back…" I managed to stifle out through my tears. He began to walk around the side of the house that I had just come from and I shook my head, sobbing even more. He got the hint without me having to explain and went around in the other direction. I could feel the blood from my cut seep down onto his arm and winced at the pain. The external pain wasn't nearly as bad as what I felt on the inside, though. I would take that any day over this.

As soon as we got around back, we neared the door and managed to get inside just as we heard a wolf's howl at the moon. He closed the door behind as he still carried me in his arms and I felt us both breathe a sigh of relief. He knew exactly where to go and headed up the stairs.

"I can walk, you know," I whispered, finally able to compose myself from before.

"I know," he nodded, continuing to carry me up and turned the doorknob to my room as we entered. As he closed the door behind us, I was placed delicately atop the bed and Calian just walked over to my wardrobe for some unknown reason. The overly modest way in which he held me to his body just a moment ago made me feel safe and warm. It was admirable the amount of self-control he had over himself to simply put me down. I had to keep looking away in an attempt to ignore the temptations to kiss him.

"Is there something you don't care about ruining in here?" he asked before touching anything within the wardrobe.

"Uhm…" I couldn't seem to remember what I even had in the wardrobe. "Anything old is fine; anything other than the dresses." He grabbed something that had fallen to the bottom underneath all the dresses and walked back over to me, gently pressing me back so that I was no longer sitting up and instead laying down on the pillow. My right leg hurt to extend it so I left it up.

"I don't want to overstep." Those deep brown eyes tugged at my heart. Yes, please overstep. My jaw clenched at the pain; I swallowed hard and pulled up the end of my nightgown to my knees. Dried blood stained the entirety of the bottom and the cut looked worse than I thought. The rock must have punctured fairly deep. He took the cup of water I had beside the bed and poured a bit on a piece of cloth, pressing it to the cut a few times. The first time, I pulled back and he stopped right away, looking up at me. Just his gaze calmed me down, but the pain was still there.

"It hurts so bad," I whispered.

"I know, but I need to clean it so it doesn't get infected," he said. "I know you must have something… alcohol? That would help."

"So you're going to get drunk?" I asked.

"No…it will clean the wound," he laughed and instantly covered his mouth, realizing it was just a bit too loud.

"Oh, it is usually down in the kitchen, but there is a small bottle in the powder room adjacent to this room. Check there." I realized how foolish I must've sounded and closed my eyes, pressing back against the bed. A few seconds later, he came back with the tiny bottle and poured some on the cloth that was already damp from the water.

"Alright, this is going to sting…" he said as I took part of the pillow and pressed my mouth against it, preparing to stifle any agony that may come out of my lips. Without warning, he tapped the cloth against my wound again and again. I groaned into the pillow at the stinging that ran through my leg. After a few more times, he finally stopped and wrapped an old shirt around the cut a few times to apply pressure.

"Thank you," I weakly moaned as I felt the world spin around me.

"Of course," he said and sat at the farthest edge of the bed from me, still beside my feet.

"I saw something out there that scared me beyond reasoning." I thought back to the graves. "Alice...she has a tombstone."

"Alice is your maid, right?" he confirmed. I nodded.

"I had just seen her earlier today, and she was fine," I said.

"Are you sure you saw her?" he asked.

"Yes. And I don't know what to do and I'm so tired yet wide awake at the same time somehow. My body feels exhausted and just needs rest, but my mind can't stop going in circles." I didn't breathe for a second and he stood up so that he was standing right over me. He knelt at my head and laced his fingers through my hair, stroking the strands down. Sometimes, there were no words for healing, just actions. One simple touch of affection said more than any words could. I tapped the bed beside me as if to ask him to lie with me.

"Are you sure?" he asked. I nodded as I hadn't been more sure of something since far before we even arrived at this wretched place.

"Cal?" I called as he walked over to the other side of the bed.

"Yeah?"

"Can you lock the door just in case?" I asked, afraid of falling asleep, then having someone find him in the morning. That was the last thing both of us needed.

"Good idea," he noted, turning around to lock the door and when I reopened my eyes, there he was lying next to me. Instead of his warm arms around me, I wrapped mine around him this time and nuzzled my head into his chest, falling into a deep sleep next to someone that I knew I was safe with, even in the horrors

of the night on Charles Island.

Morning Of

21

During the night, I woke a few times since I thought I heard a tapping on the window, but it just turned out to be the rain. Every single moment, he was there by my side and hadn't left. I took the time he was asleep to take in his handsome face. Cal's strong jawline outlined his delicate eyes, that were now closed. Strands of dark hair draped over his shoulder. I thought about him with Kitchi and how he was able to calm her down enough to allow me to come closer. And then the time that he had been here waiting during one of the most horrific nights of my life.

A sudden knock came at the door. Unlike the maids' morning knocks, it was much harsher and more relentless. It could only be one person.

"It's the big day! Rise and shine!" Father exclaimed as I watched Calian's eyes burst open in shock.

"Thank goodness you locked the door," I whispered at him as he got up and began straightening his clothes up, making the bed where he previously lay.

"You alive in there?" Father was still on the other side of the door.

"Yes, Father!" I groaned, following Calian's lead and straightening my side of the bed as well. I felt myself sink down at the end, unable to find the motivation to get myself back up. Father's loud steps revealed his departure that I was at least thankful for in the time being.

"The maids…they are gone," I said, remembering the gravestones that I saw the night before.

"We'll figure this out. Just one thing at a time," Calian assured me as he sat beside me. There wasn't much else for him to do, being that he would be caught if he tried leaving now.

"They were to prepare the dishes for this evening. I haven't the slightest idea how to make everything," I mumbled.

"Hey, I know how to cook!" he blurted out. I couldn't help but smile at his suggestion. How would I be able to talk Father into this?

"You know what? Okay. I think I will take you up on that offer," I said, thankfully. Cal started toward the window and lifted it open, pushing one leg out.

"What are you doing?!" I nearly screamed, rushing to his side. Surprisingly, my leg didn't hurt much at all and I was able to get over there without groaning in pain.

"I'm going to knock on the door in a little while and we can introduce me as the cook to your father." He must have had the idea instantaneously.

"But you'll fall," I said, tugging on his arm to come back in.

"How do you think I got in here that night?" he asked, pushing both his legs out the window so he was on the porch that surrounded the second floor. If it weren't for that, he would've surely fallen and broken all of his bones. How he planned on reaching the ground floor, I had no idea. There had to be a simpler way than this, although he seemed quite stubborn and persistent. "Go get ready. I'll be back later tonight."

"Okay, please be careful." I watched as he gracefully leapt onto the other side of the railing and began his descent. I felt as though my feet were planted on the floor as I stared outside at where he just was. What just happened? I had a handsome man in my bed last night who had enough respect to keep his hands to himself, and he just leapt out of my window. This man of which I barely knew anything about will be a cook at the event tonight where I'm supposed to be a date to an absolute monster. My life had surely become interesting, to say the least.

"Madam!" A voice that I thought I would never hear again called from the other side of the door as a few gentle knocks came. I felt my heart begin to race, so much so I thought it would jump out of my chest.

"Alice?" My voice broke as I said her name. I heard the doorknob jiggle since it was still locked from before. As I stood there watching it shake slightly, I debated jumping out the window too, as Calian just did. Although, clumsy me would surely break my bones.

"Yeah, let me in. I'm going to help you get ready," she explained, as if everything was completely normal. She already heard me answer back and clearly knew nothing about what I saw the previous night. The only way to get answers was to at least try to ask. I walked over and unlocked the door, opening it for her. Alice looked just as perfect as she had yesterday. Still no bruising visible on her face, but her hair was no longer concealed by the bonnet that she usually wore. Instead, her long blonde locks hung down over the beige dress she wore.

"Okay." I pressed my lips together in confusion and stepped toward the vanity, taking my seat. She followed and began playing with my hair, combing out the wretched mess it had been from the night before.

"What happened to your leg?" She knelt down by my side and picked up the bit of my nightgown that was a darkened red now, stained by the blood I lost.

"Oh, I tripped," I simply said. No explanation was needed...I just tripped. People trip all the time, right? Well, especially if they are me, anyway.

"This looks pretty bad. Did you clean the wound?" She unwrapped the shirt that Calian had originally placed around it.

"Yeah, it's okay." I tried to just shrug it off but watched to see what it looked like underneath once she was done unraveling the 'bandage.' It wasn't bleeding any longer, which meant whatever Calian did really helped. Around the outside, the skin was slowly scabbing to heal over the cut.

"You did this yourself?" she asked. I just shrugged my shoulders. I was a horrible liar, but if I didn't say anything, then she would believe whatever was implied. That didn't seem to count. "Well, okay. I'm going to wrap this again with something more clean. I'll be right back." She went straight out the door and I was thankful to be alone for a few more moments. The first thing I did was open the leftmost drawer on the top of the vanity and I pulled out the opal necklace I frequented. I placed it on my neck and clasped the back as I had done a plethora of times. On the windowsill that was still open, the little blackbird appeared and seemed to be looking right at me. It had the same orange patch that the other did earlier, making me think it was the same bird. I smiled, thinking of the note mother had left me in my journal that said I would receive signs.

"Okay, I've got it." The bird took off in a hurry and Alice came back to my side, rewrapping the wound.

"Alice?" I asked, able to actually get her whole name out this time without my voice breaking.

"Yes?" she asked from below.

"I saw a tombstone with your name on it." It all came out at once. I couldn't seem to hold my tongue any longer. At first, all was quiet, other than the chirping birds from outside. In the next moment, she had finished caring for my wound and stood up to look me straight in the eyes.

"Oh yes, that was just bought from before..." she answered. I felt like it was a lie, but I couldn't remember the date that it said on the tomb. I didn't even remember seeing a date, come to think of it.

"What do you mean?" I questioned.

"The previous owner made sure that we would have graves all set if the time ever came," she replied, smoothing out my hair. It didn't make much sense. Who would buy tombstones for their maids and other staff? I took a deep breath and was at least relieved that Alice was still here. Upon seeing the graves, I had thought she was dead.

"So, what do you think you're going to wear for the event?" She changed the subject. As I rummaged through the wardrobe, I came across a dress that I was given from Mother long ago. It was a yellow dress that trailed in the back. The neckline came just above my chest and was lined with a thicker ribboning that led out to the short sleeves. As I took it down and began to step into it, I remembered how refreshing it felt as the sleeves draped off my shoulders. The same thick yellow ribbon wrapped around my waistline as the remainder of the dress on my torso and below the waist was a matching shade, adorned in an elegant gold design. The intricate details of golden leaves sewn on along a vine spread over almost the entirety of the dress.

"It's beautiful," Alice remarked. "Everyone is going to love it."

"Thank you. I'm so glad you're okay." I felt a tear stream down my cheek and realized it was too late to conceal it.

"Of course I am! Why wouldn't I be?" she laughed, and we headed down the steps with just a few hours lingering until everyone would start piling in.

Arrival

22

When the time for the event neared, I had been upstairs applying powder and straighten my hair for the evening. Father had come up to tell me of the new chef that we'd be using for the night.

"Angeline…oh you look so much like your mother many years ago." He held his hand to his heart. "That's her dress, too!" He came over to me as I still sat in front of the mirror, placing small pieces of lilies of the valley in various parts of my hair that was back in a braided bun.

"Thank you." I kissed his cheek and got back to what I was doing.

"Oh, and I don't know how you did it, but thank you for finding a chef for the night. He should be of great help to Alice and Mary," he confirmed that Calian had made it in. I felt my heart stop at the very thought that he was so close and in the same house.

"I agree." I was glad that he seemed to like him.

"How did you find him?" The question that I definitely feared the most. I couldn't lie to Father.

"On the mainland. I found that he was able to cook and knew we were running out of time to find staff." I smiled at Father through the mirror and he made eye contact back.

"So that's why you were so late to come back that day and even took the paddle boat back this way." He put the pieces together that I very much didn't want him to.

"Maybe." I shrugged my shoulders. He might as well gone to become a policeman or detective.

"You like him, huh?" he finished the puzzle.

"Pfft, Dad…just because he's a guy…" I trailed off and occupied myself by placing the opal earrings in my ears.

"I am fine with you being with anyone as long as they can take care of you." It was a great surprise to my ears. It was greatly frowned upon for both of us to be together, yet Father didn't seem to care.

"Really?"

"You're better off with him than some nut like George. Which speaking of…have you heard from him?" His face began to grow red at the mention of him.

"No, I haven't. But please let's not bring up anything. We need to just remain civil and calm, at least for tonight," I reminded him. He grunted and began walking away. "Thanks, Father! Love you!" I called out after him.

"Calian…the chef…I gave him a suit that I used to fit into when I was younger…" He rubbed his belly and mumbled something upon leaving the room. I got up and walked over to him, hugging him as tight as I could.

"Thank you, I really appreciate it." He returned the hug.

"Gotta go get dressed myself! You sure I can't just hide over in the office?" he joked. I slapped him playfully on the arm and followed after him, heading down the steps so that I could make sure everything was together for our guests. But I more-so wanted to go check on Calian in the kitchen. He must have been as spooked as I seeing that Alice and Mary were still here after all when I had just told him they had died. As I went down the stairs, I could hear laughter beaming from the kitchen. It sounded like Alice's voice. I headed in that direction to find Calian and her, both busy as bees. Alice was plating the food while he continued cooking. The pitchers of tea looked all ready to be brought out.

"Angeline!" Alice called out as I made my way in, tasting one of the small slices of bread with jelly spread on its side.

"Mmm, this is delicious!" I was surprised to see the two of them in such good spirits. "You'll have to teach me how to cook someday." I looked over at Calian, then back at Alice. "Thank you both for helping with this. I really mean it."

"So, Alice seemed to know all about me..." Calian noted, and I felt the heat spread across my face.

"I was glad to finally put a face to the name!" Alice wasn't helping at all... "I think he's a keeper for you." Be. Quiet. Alice.

"I'm glad you got to meet each other finally! Both of my good friends here together!" I exclaimed, ignoring the sudden spotlight that was set on me.

"Oh, you two going to be okay on your own? I've got to go grab something from the pantry," Alice called over her shoulder upon leaving the room. It was a rhetorical question. She knew the answer, but just seemed to want to make me squirm even more. So this is what it was like to have a sister...

"You look..." Cal began walking over to me, "like a budding flower at dawn just when the morning dew has glossed over its petals."

"And you look quite handsome yourself." I couldn't help but smile at the apron he wore over a shirt he must have borrowed from Father as well. He still wore the beige slacks that he normally wore.

"I couldn't put on the dress clothes yet," he admitted and looked down. "I would surely get stains on it from cooking in here."

"That was thoughtful," I assured him.

"So, I'm assuming Alice is alright?" he asked.

"I guess so! Things seem to get crazier by the minute here," I sighed, and a few sudden knocks sounded in the once silent air. I checked the clock, and it was just around five forty-five p.m. Still fifteen minutes until the guests were set to arrive. Cal kissed me on the forehead and got back to his work so that I could get the door. Upon leaving the room, I briefly passed by Alice, who looked spooked. Just a few moments ago, she had been in great spirits and laughing with us like some children… I wondered what caused the change. When I tried to stop her to ask, she just increased her pace back into the kitchen and the knocks came a second time, impatiently.

"Yes, yes! I'm coming!" I yelled out and grabbed the sides of my dress to hold them up so as not to trip over them as I raced toward the door.

"Lady Angeline." George's eyes shone upon entering the house. He took my hand and kissed the back of it, releasing it right after.

"Fellow, she may be your date tonight but don't forget she's still my daughter." Father saved me from the inevitable doom. A threatening look came across George's face, but it quickly faded and was masked by his fake smile.

"Yes, sir," he said.

"Here, let me lead you to the ballroom. I want to make sure everything is set up because we just have a few minutes left," I told George and as he set out for the ballroom before me. Father and I exchanged a brief look. I mouthed to him 'I'm Ok' and he just shook his head, walking over towards the office.

As George and I went into the ballroom, there was such an extensive amount of decor. Around the room were candles on the walls that had already been carefully lit. Several small tables surrounded the perimeter of the room, and each had a few chairs. At the centers were small vases that contained a single flower in each. I looked over at the last table and saw Mary placing a flower in the once empty vase. I left George by the entrance to the room and walked over to Mary.

"This all looks so amazing, Mary. Did you do this?" I asked. She looked up at me with her tired eyes and smiled, nodding her head.

"I had some help from Calian and Alice," she remarked. I wondered how long Calian had even been there for.

"Ehem," George cleared his throat, bringing both our attention over toward him. I gave a departing smile to Mary as I reluctantly headed back to George.

"What's wrong?" I asked. "Oh, do you want to hang up your coat in the coatroom?"

"Yes, can you show me the way?" he asked. He knows this house better than I, so it was strange that he had to ask me where it was.

"Okay." I started walking through the middle of the ballroom and came to a door on the other side, opening it to reveal a small room with many hooks and shelves in the back. "I can take it."

"Thank you." He peeled his coat off himself and draped it over my arm as I walked into the dark room. If not for the small window that let in the sun, I wouldn't have been able to find anything in here. This was a room that I hadn't frequented and wished I did more often because the guests would've surely wanted to put their coats up as well. I put the jacket on an open hook and turned around, instantly being pushed back up against the wall. The door to the ballroom had been closed and just when I thought George had stayed there, he was instead pressing his body up against mine.

"What are you doing?" I asked, attempting to push him off me. I felt his sweaty hand grip my breast as he continued pressing me back against the wall. I was cornered and had no way out. He kissed my cheek and just when he was about to plant his lips onto mine, I heard Father call from the ballroom.

"The guests have arrived!"

The Grand Opening

23

As soon as Father interrupted George of whatever he had been doing, I took the physical mask that I had been holding and placed it over my face, masking half of my appearance. It felt all too suiting due to the fact that I have had to put on a metaphorical mask on frequent occasions and pretend to be someone that I was not. George was in a hurry to walk out first and I overheard him agreeing to welcome in the guests. As I pressed my ear to the door, I could hear Father telling him to take a seat and saying that it was my job to greet them all. I smirked and wished I could give him a hug just for that. George's expression must have been priceless. I no longer had any sympathy for him after what he just tried to do without so much as my consent. He seemed to think he owned the entire world around him just because he had all the money one could ever dream of. I walked out of the coat closet to find George talking with the musician. I couldn't help but clench my jaws at the mere sight of him...as I continued out the ballroom, I neared the foyer to find at least a dozen guests all adorned in their own exquisite masks. Each woman was accompanied by their date and around half of them looked my age, but the remainder were far older and just about Father's age. Father had refused to wear a mask, but introduced me anyway.

"Everyone, this is my daughter, Lady Angeline. She worked endlessly to put all of this together." He held out his hand, and I curtsied toward everyone. The men bowed as the women mirrored me. In the very front was a girl with a plain gold mask on, if not for the elaborate feathers protruding from the side of it. I wondered how it even stayed on her all the way. Her ruby lips stood out against the pale shade of her skin. The green dress she wore was much more elaborate than my own and she had the curves to fill it. Her wavy brunette hair was simply laid down against her back with a delicate strand laying over her chest. The man she was with seemed to match her ensemble, in that he had a dark green vest on, with a white shirt underneath and dark green trousers. They looked to be around my age...maybe just a few years older, but nearly the same. Behind them, everyone else had a variety of colors they wore, including on their choice of mask. The two seemed to lead the rest.

"Come this way." I showed them to the ballroom and upon entering, the music was already playing a peaceful melody of the violin along with some piano. There had been several musicians at the very back of the room, each stationed at their own instrument. From behind me, I heard several oohs and ahs in amazement at the delight this evening turned out to be for them at least.

"Make yourselves comfortable. We have tables around that you can sit at and some food will be around, too." I curtsied as if to bid my farewell upon leaving them to find themselves at home. When I looked over at the musicians again, I noticed George wasn't even there. I scanned the room and couldn't seem to find him. After walking around to each table and asking if anyone needed anything, I saw Father laughing away with the guests that seemed closer to his age.

"Hey Dad," I whispered beside him.

"Yes, Ange?" He excused himself from the table and we walked over to the side.

"Any idea where George went off to?" I asked, already nervous about what he could've been up to. Father shrugged his shoulders. "Okay, I'm going to go check on everyone in the kitchen and I'll be right back." He went back to the same table that he had just been at and seemed to carry on the conversation where he had left off.

As I walked in, Alice was just on her way out with a pitcher of tea in each hand.

"Thank you," she said as she walked out through the door I had just opened.

"Anytime," I replied and walked fully in. Mary was cleaning the dishes at the sink while Cal began cleaning things up. It seemed that he was just about done since there were platters full of various foods awaiting to be brought out.

"How is it in there so far?" he asked. Although I had a mask on the upper portion of my face, I couldn't conceal the way that I felt around him and just frowned, sitting down at a stool beside the cupboard. "That bad, huh?"

"He came onto me and now I can't seem to find him anywhere," I said.

"Can't seem to find who?" A voice came in from the other side of the kitchen, just through the doorway. George wandered in and took my hand, forcing me to stand up all the way. At first, it looked as though Calian was about to lunge forward, but he pressed his hand against the handle of a knife and just stared.

"Oh, there you are. Everyone has arrived. Let's head back in," I said as he completely ignored me and just stared down at Cal. It was similar to two dogs from entirely different packs as they threatened one another with their mere presence. Cal broke his gaze from George and looked at me, then headed back to the stove that he was now closing the flame and cleaning.

"Yes, let's go back in." George purposefully kissed my cheek while we were still in the kitchen and I could feel the tension between Cal and him as it radiated through the air. As we exited the kitchen and re-entered the ballroom, I briefly turned to look back at Cal and his usual glowing and vibrant face was now looking sullen and dark.

"What was that all about?" I asked George as he held my hand, pulling me toward the center of the ballroom. Several of the couples were up and dancing, switching partners as they swayed about the room. We joined in the middle and George kept hold of my hand while placing his other on my side. I felt myself flinch at his touch, which was a bit more delicate than before.

"Who was that in there?" he asked.

"The cook…" I answered the obvious question.

"He wasn't part of my staff when I owned this place." He swayed me back as to follow everyone else's moves and brought me up again, continuing to move from side to side about the room.

"Okay." There was not much else to say to that. Just because he didn't have him working there didn't mean that we couldn't ever hire more staff. I didn't have to explain who Calian truly was in the slightest.

"I saw the eyes he has for you. But it's too bad because you are already mine." The last few words that came out of his mouth sent chills down my spine. I felt like the longer I knew George, the more I was able to see the true beast within him.

"I am not yours..." I clenched my jaw, no longer wanting to wear the mask that I had for so long. As if it was perfect timing, it was our cue to switch partners, and I yanked my hand out of his grasp, drifting off to another man. This man was the one who had accompanied the lady in green from earlier in the foyer. His light brown hair was wavy and went down to just below his ears.

"Edward," he introduced himself briefly. He was a quiet one, but I didn't mind it because it was more enjoyable to be able to listen to the music. But more than that, it was heavenly being away from George. At each turn, I caught a slight glimpse of him and he looked quite angered. I switched partners a few more times and ended up with another man that was much taller than I. I didn't remember seeing him before, but unlike many of the other masks, his nearly covered his entire face. It was pure white and had gold designs of leaves all over the mask. He had black hair, although I couldn't quite tell since it seemed tied back. Unlike the others, he did not introduce himself. He just grasped his left arm on my waist and took my hand in his own. It seemed like it was this man's first time dancing since I seemed to lead the way and at times, I struggled to keep my own feet away from nearly being stepped on.

"Do you know how to dance?" I asked, trying not to be rude, but also genuinely interested. He shook his head, and I laughed. "Then why are you here?"

"You," he returned. As we made our way past one of the candles in the dimly lit room, I looked directly into his eyes and saw the familiar chestnut brown staring back at me.

"Calian?" I whispered, looking over my shoulder to make sure George couldn't hear. He was dancing with another partner, but still looking my way, as he probably had the entire night. The outfit must've been borrowed from Father. Although it was fitting, it was also a little short on the length of his pants since he was taller than father…but it still worked. His toned body was revealed just as much from wearing the jacket.

"Shh," he said and seemed to get better the more we danced. When the other men dipped their partner, I signaled him to do the same.

"Okay, pull me up now and we continue what we were doing before," I directed him. It was time to switch partners, and I was sure that George would be the next one to match with me, but Calian just continued holding on to me, leading me away from him. Upon turning, I could see George was stuck with another partner and he had a look of defeat on his face.

"He's going to know," I whispered.

"Then let him," he replied, and this time, he led me around the room. At one point, he lifted my hand up in the air and twirled me around. I felt my dress whirl and could also tell most eyes were on me in the room. The music ended, and I saw Father walk up to the front of the room, clapping. Cal squeezed my hand tight and walked away toward the other side of the room. I felt George's presence take his place.

"Everyone, thank you for coming! We will now have the drawing of our guests that will win the night at our resort!" Father yelled out as everyone clapped for him in excitement. I peered over at George and could tell he was not interested in the winning at all, but instead holding me prisoner in his grasp as he clenched my hand, nearly making me lose feeling in my fingers.

Reflection

24

"Come on, Ange!" All eyes looked toward me as Father called out my name. I glanced up at George and he seemed to reluctantly give up my hand as I shook it, trying to gain feeling again. When I got up beside Father, he put his arm around me and plastered a big, embarrassing kiss on my cheek.

"I know, I know… you're not five years old anymore…" Our audience laughed in unison.

"Alright, let's see who won the stay tonight!" I put my hand in the bowl and started stirring all the papers about as to make a fair chance for everyone

"The first winner goes to.... " The crowd was completely silent; only my voice echoed in the room. I picked up the nearly crumpled paper and read the name aloud. "Anna!" The lady in dark green walked up to me and I shook her hand.

"Wow, I didn't think I'd actually win!" she exclaimed and seemed to hop back with excitement to her partner.

"Congratulations, Anna! We have two more lucky winners! The next one goes to..." I shuffled the papers around even more and took out another piece. "Patrick!" The very quiet man that I had danced with right after George took slow steps and shook my hand.

"Thank you," he mumbled under his breath.

"Yes, of course!" As he walked back to join the crowd, I gave the papers once last stir in the bowl with my hand and squeezed my eyes shut extra tight to show I wasn't cheating. "The last free stay goes to..." I picked out a torn piece of paper that was much unlike the others. The writing was very difficult to make out although it was only three letters. As the distorted *A* seemed to be combined with the next letter, I could finally make it out.

"Cal!" Everyone cheered for the winners, except for George, who stood in the back, arms crossed over his chest. Cal came up and shook my hand and Father came to shake his hand too.

"To the winners...congratulations! You will be staying at the resort free of charge tonight. Mary can show you to your room upstairs. Thank you for coming out to support our inn! We will see you off as the sun is just setting and you need to get home before dark. Thank you again!" I was glad Father shooed them out because the sun was in fact reaching the horizons. I saw Mary at the ballroom's exit and she welcomed the two pairs of winners. There was only one winner missing, and it was Cal. I glanced over at Father and saw that he was talking with him. Cal had already taken off the mask he had on earlier. On the other side of the room where George had just stood, it was now empty. I scanned around each corner and couldn't place where he went.

"Have either of you seen where George went off to?" I asked, wishing I knew he had at least left the island.

"Oh, that little rich boy threw a tantrum and then took off. He's long gone by now; I saw his boat leave the shores." I breathed a sigh of relief. "I was just over here offering Calian a more permanent job."

"I appreciate your offer very much, but I have my people to get back to." Cal shook Father's hand.

"Are you going to at least stay the night?" I asked, hopeful. Before he could answer, Father took a step forward.

"Of course he has to! He won a free stay; who wouldn't claim that? Come on, let's get you over to Mary so that she can show you to your room. I think she just left the ballroom to head upstairs." Father put his arm around Cal and led him away from me. He looked over his shoulder at me with worry in his eyes. Cal always had the same look on his face when he had to leave my side, but I somehow felt safer that he would at least be under the same roof tonight.

"Hey, you've had a long day, madam…" I felt someone gently touch my shoulder and looked over to see Alice.

"I think I'm ready for bed after all this," I said, wishing there was a bed right beside me that I could just fall onto.

"Alright, let's get you ready for sleep," she said. I looked around at everything still out in the room and she seemed to read my mind. "No worries, we will have this cleaned up tonight."

When we passed by a window, I could see the glow from the sliver of sunlight that remained as dusk quickly approached. Upstairs, the guests were already in their rooms with the doors closed. All was silent, as if they too had fallen into a deep slumber. I looked at each door and wondered which one led to Cal, but we just continued past the rooms and into my own. The first thing I did was peel myself out of the yellow dress that I had on just about the entire day. With how clumsy I was, it was surprising that I hadn't dripped a single drop on the fabric and it remained the same as it was earlier. I threw it over the changing wall and slipped on a nightgown.

"This was such a beautiful dress," Alice exclaimed, taking it off the changing wall to hang up for a proper cleaning later.

"Thank you, it was my mother's," I revealed.

"You know, there's one in your wardrobe that I have never seen you wear. It's that white one."

"That also belonged to Mother. I'm saving it for my wedding someday," I admitted, sighing at the fact that it seemed nowhere close.

"You would make a beautiful bride," she revealed. I looked down at the ground and breathed in deeply, heading over to the powder room that was on the side of my bedroom. The only entrance to it was from in here, so it at least gave me more privacy. There was no need to close the door behind me because I was only looking at my face in the mirror, wiping off the powder and blush with a wet rag.

"Someday…" I said as I splashed water on my face.

"It'll happen. You've just got to keep looking on the bright side," she reminded me and walked up from behind to comb my hair out of the braided bun it had previously been in. As I looked in the mirror, I could only see myself. I moved to the side and still saw the same reflection, as if Alice wasn't actually behind me at all. I had only a little bit to drink, but nowhere close to the amount that would mess up my mind that badly.

"Where are you?" I asked, puzzled.

"Right here," she answered. I whipped around and saw that she was still there with the comb in her hands.

"But I don't see your reflection in the mirror and you were right behind me," I said.

"You probably had too much to drink..."

"No, Alice. I didn't see you there. You have no reflection in the mirror, haven't left this island and you have a tombstone with your name on it. Something isn't right." I started putting the pieces together aloud.

"Why don't you just get some rest and we can talk about this in the morning," she insisted as she walked away toward the door to leave the room. I followed after her and grabbed her arm, my hand seemingly going straight through it.

"You're not here," I realized.

"Oh, don't be silly. I am right in front of you — use your eyes!" she laughed nervously.

"Alice…just tell me the truth."

"The truth…" she sighed and sat at the edge of my bed. "If I tell you, you promise not to run?"

"I already feel like running now, so what's the difference?" I asked.

"Fair point. The truth is that I am not entirely sure how it happened, but one morning I had been feeling aches and pains all over my body. I fell into a peaceful sleep and then woke up feeling better than I ever had before," she started. I lifted my eyebrows as if to say 'and…?'

"Well, the day was going quite normal from there until I entered the powder room and realized the same as you had. I ran to get mother right away, and she seemed to know. She stood in front of the mirror too and we saw that both of our reflections were completely gone.

"Mother explained to me that it happened to her a while ago and she never told me because she thought it would upset me. So there I was, always cooking beside her and never truly knowing what was going on…All she said was to stay away from George and I did." She stopped and looked my way.

"So what does this mean?" I asked, feeling as if I had, in fact, drank too much wine.

"I died."

"But then, how do I see you?" She had to be joking. I thought of how I saw James, who was supposedly dead, but he seemed much different than Alice. Much more malevolent.

"There is a curse on this island from long ago and whoever dies stays within its territory."

"How is this possible?"

"You're asking me? I don't quite know." She seemed as frustrated as I was.

"So then you can never leave?"

"I don't think so…but if someone on the mainland has something of ours, then I can appear wherever that is."

I sat in the open space on the bed and felt myself fall back, wishing again that it could just swallow me whole. Nothing was making sense and if I tried relaying this information to anyone, I would surely end up in the nuthouse.

"How did it happen?"

"I don't know," she answered and left me lying in bed, tormented by the thoughts. As she left, she made sure to lock the door from the inside. "Try to get some rest, ok? Goodnight."

Creature in the Night

25

That night, I lay restless again…tempted to check each door to see where Cal was staying. I closed my eyes, and the thoughts raced through my mind of Alice… Mary… and James. How could it be? It was one thing to have nightmares about the impossible, but to actually be awake while the unexplainable occurred? I tried taking deep breaths, but nothing seemed to stop it. I thought of the night that Cal laid beside me after wrapping my wound and how peaceful his face looked. I squeezed my own shut and tried to imagine that he was there right next to me. I somehow fell into a deep sleep, holding the pillow in my arms.

When I awoke, it was still night, and all was dark within the room. No candles were lit, and even the full moon must have been hidden behind clouds as darkness crept through the windows. I readjusted and moved my pillow on the other side of me, rolling over. Just then, the doorknob jiggled. I wondered if it was Cal, wishing to go over there and open it up for him. But there was also a chance that it wasn't him and I would be met with something horrific that I had so carefully locked myself up from. It could've been one of the guests not remembering where their room was... I decided to stay in bed, pulling the covers over my face.

In the next second, the doorknob jiggled again and then I heard a metallic sound as it clicked into place from the other side of the door and turned. It was someone who had a key.

I just lay there and made sure not to make a sound. If it was dark in here, they wouldn't be able to see me as well. They closed the door behind them and entered my room. This would be the perfect time for the bed to open up from underneath and swallow me. I saw a glimmer of light from a candle that they must've brought in. It would no longer conceal the fact that I was there. I squeezed my eyes shut one last time and sat up, allowing the covers to fall down to my lap. The tall, slender body of a man was already right beside me as he set down the candle in the holder along the wall.

"George?" I blurted out, loud enough that it caused him more irritation.

"Shh," he whispered as he pinned me down to the bed, stopping me from being able to escape. His hair was wet, as if he had just been swimming and was dripping onto me, causing me to shiver. I felt the goosebumps creep up and down my arms from his cold touch.

"Get out," I sternly said as he pressed his lips into mine, stopping me from being able to say anything else. He pushed the sheets down me more and brought his hand to cover my mouth as he began kissing down my neck. I twisted and turned my body, but it only caused him to press into me more with his. His lips made their way down my chest and body until he seemed unable to hold himself back any longer and ripped at the sheets, lifting my nightgown up so that there was no longer anything stopping him.

His hand came off my mouth and I let out a scream before he was able to cover my mouth once more with his hand. I felt the pillow that I had been holding the entire night as he put it over my face to stifle my yells. I gasped for air as both of my legs were moved to the side and I heard him loosen his trousers pushing into me. I felt myself lose consciousness and the entire world around me went black.

"Angeline? Angeline, are you okay?" A soft, gentle voice woke me. My blanket was up to my neck, covering nearly my entire body. I blinked a few times and saw Cal standing on the other side of me, the same worry in his eyes as he always had when leaving. But it didn't look as though he would be leaving this time.

"What happened?" I asked, looking on the other side of the bed to find George's limp body laying there. I shrieked and jumped out of bed. "Oh, my God. Oh, my God. Why is he there?"

"You don't remember what he did to you?" Calian asked. I blinked a few moments and tried to break down the wall that I had clearly already put up in my mind.

"Well, last night, I remember locking the door and then he just let himself in with the key. He tried kissing me...and I told him to get off. Then, oh my God." I looked down at my ripped nightgown that barely covered me and wrapped the blanket that I tore from the bed around myself more. There was a distinct pain between my legs that I had never felt before, and it was almost throbbing.

"I knew something wasn't right. I was coming from the balcony outside to enter the room and that's when I saw him over you. He would have suffocated you to death." I could hear the anger in his voice. He said the last sentence through gritted teeth.

"So, you killed him?" I took a few steps back toward the bed, seeing a knife impaled into his back. George was laying face down as if he had just been rolled off of me. The blood seeped through my white bed sheets around where his torso lay.

"What other choice did I have?" Cal asked, walking in front of me to block my view of the scene. "Are you ok?" And when he asked those three words, I felt myself completely lose it. The wall that I had put up in my mind was there for a reason. Because I couldn't take the thought of having been taken advantage of in that way.

Having been touched by some animal after I squirmed helplessly underneath. I felt like I had been a bunny, unable to see their predator coming and brutally torn up from the insides. My legs gave out from underneath me and I fell into Cal's arms. He sat on the bed and held me close to his chest, rubbing my back in circles without saying a word. Because even he knew, there were no words for this.

"I was too late." His voice dropped into a depressed tone.

"If you were too late, I'd be dead." I swallowed hard and wiped my tears, looking at him right in his sweet, brown eyes.

"I should've never let him lay a hand on you."

"It's not your fault. He's a monster." I peered over at George's body that still lay there. The sun was just peeking over the horizons as light filtered through the windows. My mind went to the guests that were staying here their first night and immediately worried about them finding out what had happened. They would call Calian a murderer and he'd surely be hanged to the death.

A knock came from the other side of my door. We both seemed to jump in place. I walked over and slightly opened the door, peeking my head out as not to allow them in. Alice stood on the other side of the doorway and appeared to be ignorant of all that happened. I thought about my talk the previous night with her and how she was brutally beaten by George just before her death. As I looked at her, my eyes widened.

"Well, you look like you saw a ghost," she laughed. Hilarious.

"Alice, come in here," I urged. Her face suddenly grew serious, and she followed me in as I quickly shut the door behind her.

"What in the world?" she exclaimed.

"Shh," Calian and I both shushed her in unison. She held a hand to her mouth.

"He broke in last night and…he did something very horrible to me. I nearly died." I looked down at my feet, not wanting to make eye contact with anyone.

"So I had no choice. He was just about to suffocate her to death when I came at him from behind. He didn't seem to expect it and when it happened, Angeline was already unconscious," Cal explained.

"Do you think…do you think he is the reason for my death, too?" Alice looked over at me and we explained it to Calian, who listened fully and didn't say much in return. I didn't know if he actually believed us or was making a mental note in his mind to ask Father about checking us into an institution…but either way, we needed to figure out what to do with George's body.

"Okay." Alice took charge. "Many of the guests have luggage. There's a rather large duffel bag that has never been used in the closet. I can go retrieve it and we can put his body in there."

"How are we going to dispose of him," I asked, "without anyone noticing…?"

"Hm…well, once all the company is gone — you keep your father occupied in the house while Cal and I bring him to the graves to bury," Alice said as Cal nodded his head in agreement. I blinked a few times as if it would help me awaken from this nightmare, but it didn't work no matter how hard I squeezed my eyes. When Alice came back with the duffel bag, Cal was the one to load his body into it while Alice ripped the sheets off the bed and loaded them into the duffel bag as well. The blood had seeped into the mattress and I noticed Alice had temporarily covered it with another blanket from the closet.

"Okay, take a deep breath and everything will be okay," Alice assured me. It was not okay in any way, shape or form…but at the very least, I was alive. I'm not sure how much that counted for on this island, anyway. I went first and as I passed the other guest rooms, all was quiet. Heading down the stairs, I looked at the clock on the wall and realized it was nearing six in the morning. I must've barely slept a wink. When I neared the dining room, I saw Father sitting down with a cup of coffee while reading the newspaper. I dropped to my knees in the doorway and began sobbing. He rushed over and held me in his arms as I told him everything that had happened.

The Meeting

26

Years went by and there had been no sign of George after that day. Although it had been quite a while since the incident, I never fully healed or was the same. At times, the wall that I put up in my mind would develop holes within it and the darkness would consume me. Those days, I wasn't quite able to leave my bed. Calian continued to come by again and again. At first, with any touch from him, I'd jump. But over time, I learned to trust that he wouldn't do anything to harm me. Alice and Mary stayed with us in the Charles Island House and we let every guest believe they were truly here. James, on the other hand…his spirit seemed to have lifted once George was no longer alive. If a spirit is angry and has unfinished business, they will often show as evil spirits. Mary and Alice, on the other hand, their business was never finished as maids in this house. It was as though they would never leave, which they seemed perfectly content with as was I. Because…in fact, humans were far scarier than any ghosts I had ever seen.

Father decided to open his button and cane making shop back up from within the home. He would frequently travel to the mainland to deliver them into town. I was glad that it kept him occupied, but there was never a dull moment where I wasn't busy. I spent most of my time with Calian aside from taking over the finances of the inn. He taught me many things, such as fishing and cooking, while I gave him lessons on how to dance without stepping on my toes. It definitely kept my mind occupied, but on some occasions, I would venture back to the mainland to give Kitchi more apples. She became so accustomed to me that instead of Calian having to pet her while I slowly crept towards her, she would come up to me and nuzzle her nose into my picnic basket, taking out an apple for herself. Since it always became expected, I never forgot to bring a sweet treat for her.

One afternoon in the fall, we planned to have a picnic on the mainland, right on the shores. Right before we left, I remember seeing Calian look at my father repeatedly as if they both knew something that I did not. I remember asking them, 'what?' And they both started giggling like a bunch of teenagers. When Calian and I arrived at the shore of the mainland, we made sure to take the paddle boat so that we could get back in case of high tide coming to conceal the path.

"Where do you want to sit?" I asked, looking for a smooth, sandy spot to drape the blanket over. He continued walking on for some reason. "Well, I guess not here!"

"Angeline, I have another place that we can have the picnic," he said.

"And where's that?"

"I want to bring you to the reservation to show you my family now that I have known yours for some time," he revealed, turning back toward me, worry in his eyes.

"Right now?" I asked, looking down at the dark green dress that I wore, not even knowing if I fully combed my hair that morning.

"You look fine. You always look beautiful." He seemed to have read my mind. "Come on, they don't bite."

"Okay, okay…lead the way!" We followed Kitchi, who had lost her white spots by now and was a doe through the bushes and past the trees. It felt like we had never been on a beach at all, being that we were now in the middle of a forest with a surplus of trees and bushes. So much so that Cal took my hand to follow him so that I followed the path he had made. Kitchi seemed to have no problem with moving along a path. It felt like it was taking forever and my feet began to ache.

"Is it in the same state?" I joked.

"Yes, yes. Just a little farther." He stopped where he was and gave me the picnic basket to hold. In the next second, he reached under my legs and scooped me up, continuing to walk through the vast forest. I started giggling at his sudden surprise and he smiled back at me. While it had once been quiet other than birds chirping and a cool fall breeze drifting through the air, I heard the crackle of a fire nearby and people's voices. I couldn't make out what they were saying, as it sounded like it was in another language.

"Okay, here we are." He set me down and there was a clearing with not traditional houses...but log homes made from tree bark. It didn't look like anything I had ever seen before. Beside two of these houses was a fire pit, fully engulfed in flames as several people who looked similar to Calian sat around it. The women's and men's hair was dark and long, just like his, and they had tanned skin that looked like it had been kissed by the sun.

"Do they know English?" I asked.

"Some of them do, but mostly no. They speak our native language," he explained.

"I will smile and nod."

He laughed and held my hand as Kitchi had walked over to one of the little kids and they began petting her. I could tell she loved every minute of the attention because her head was up in the air and she just stayed still to let them continue. Cal and I approached the fire pit and stared at a lady who was sitting beside it, her hands gaining its warmth. Her gray hair looked thick and healthy; she stood up right away and put both of her hands out, wrapping them around me in a hug. I glanced at Cal and he just smiled at both of us.

"That's my Nookomis. Grandmother," he revealed.

"It's very nice to meet you," I mustered out, even though I wasn't sure she understood me. When she pulled away, she just smiled and nodded. She had a bag with her and opened it up, pulling out a rounded circle that had netting within. Feathers hung down from the bottom of the circle.

"A dream catcher. It will help to make sure you do not have anymore nightmares," he said. I suddenly realized that Calian must've told his family all about me. My cheeks felt red. I took the gift from her and nodded, smiling. I could tell that Calian was closest with his grandmother since she was the first that he had introduced me to.

The next person who I met looked nearly identical to Calian, except he had a much more rigid look. He was slightly older, his hair more choppy and eyes much darker. I held out my hand as if to shake his.

"I am Calian's brother, Etu." He took my hand and shook it.

"I am Angeline," I said while I smiled.

"Etu means the sun. What does Angeline mean?" he asked. I hesitated for a moment.

"It was my grandmother's name and Father gave it to me so that her spirit could live on in me through her name," I said. He nodded and seemed to appreciate that. Out of the corner of my eye, I could see Calian's grandmother nodding too.

"Etu will be chief," Cal said as he slapped his brother on the back. Etu smiled mischievously and slapped him harder, only for Cal to do it again and begin running around the firepit like a bunch of children. I couldn't hold back my laughter. If I thought there was no one more muscular than Cal, I was wrong, because what appeared to be the chief stood up before me and the boys stopped playing around at once. He had various red and black markings about his body.

"My name is Achak; named after my great-great-grandfather, meaning spirit, much like his name meant as well." I don't know why, but I felt the need to bow before him. When I did this, they all started laughing, including Achak.

"Well, it is very nice to meet you. I take it you are Calian's father?" I asked, trying to ignore the laughs, although I felt like I could join them.

"Yes, and this is my wife, Aiyana." He grasped the hand of one of the most beautiful women I had ever seen. She had the same brown hair as Calian and Etu, but also light blue eyes. I couldn't understand it because everyone else in the tribe seemed to have some shade of brown. She gave a gentle smile my way. Just then, everyone stopped talking and sat around the fire pit, staring at Calian and I. I hadn't realized that he made his way back over by my side, but he looked the most nervous I had ever seen him. He got down on one knee and pulled out a small, velvety bag that had been tied in a bow with string. It looked vaguely familiar, but I couldn't place it. When Cal undid the string, he pulled out a gold ring with a diamond in the center. Two small emeralds lined either side of the diamond and it matched Mother's necklace perfectly that I barely ever wore.

"Angeline, I wanted to bring you to the most special place so that I could do this. I know that this is the custom with your family and…Angeline, will you marry me?" His puppy-dog eyes looked up at me and I felt like my lips were sewn shut. Just when I felt like everyone's eyes were on both of us, it suddenly felt like we were the only two people in the entire world. I felt a tear stream down my cheek. This is what he and Father were snickering about earlier. Father must have given him the ring and his approval.

"Yes, oh my God, yes, Calian."

I got down on my knees beside him and he slipped the ring on my finger. It felt like a waterfall on my face as the tears came down all at once. We hugged there while kneeling and everyone in his tribe cheered for us. For the remainder of the afternoon, we danced around the fire and this time he showed me how to do their traditional dance.

Wedding Day

27

The day that I felt like I had waited for my entire life was finally here. I hadn't slept a wink the night before and kept pacing over to the wardrobe to look at Mother's dress that I intended on wearing. It was made entirely of white lace and had several ruffles at the very bottom, leading to a short trail in the back. The top was thicker than the rest of the dress, in that the upper portion of its sleeves were ruffled down to a slim lace that extended to the remainder of my arms. Alice had come into my room that morning and was surprised to see me already busy at the vanity, applying a meager amount of blush on my cheeks and leaving the powder out completely. Over the past few years, Calian had made it known on several occasions that I was much more beautiful with my natural skin. It felt like a big change to leave the room without it, but I became used to it and my skin actually felt better, too, without much on it. Growing comfortable in my own skin was something I had to learn to do, and Cal was there to help me every step of the way. I pulled open the bottom drawer and carefully took out the Victorian emerald necklace with its diamond pattern that matched the ring he had proposed with. As I began clasping the back, I felt Alice's presence near me and take it in her own hands. She had no trouble doing so since it was on in a matter of seconds. I used the gold earrings from the middle drawer and then took out the photo of Mother.

"Wow, I see where you get your beauty from." Alice and I had become very good friends to the point that she knew she could say anything to me.

"Thank you," I said, about to wipe a tear from my cheek.

"No, no!" she yelled, taking a handkerchief to wipe it instead. "You'll dirty that gorgeous white dress of yours!"

"You're right," I laughed. "I guess we better get me to this wedding rather quick or I will surely walk in with a stain-covered dress." She laughed as she toyed with my hair.

"You know what? I saw something in the wardrobe."

"What might that be?" I asked, curious.

"Hang on." She walked over to wardrobe and opened it up, pulling out a white lace hat that seemed to match perfectly with my gown. In her other hand was an umbrella adorned in the same fashion.

"What!" I exclaimed, jumping out of my seat.

"You mean to tell me you never knew of these things??" She placed the hat down on the vanity and leaned the closed umbrella against the wall. I shrugged my shoulders as she began to put my hair up.

"Can you do it like this?" I handed Alice the photo of Mother so that she could see the interwoven bun that she did her hair in that day. It looked beautiful because it was quite loose, some hair even draped down slightly at the sides as all the strands came back together in the bun.

"I will try my best."

I kept my eyes closed so that it could be a surprise to me once she was done and when I felt the hat being placed on my head, I opened them back up to find that I did, in fact, look just like mother. Father was bound to cry. As I felt the tear stream down my face, Alice was already on it with the handkerchief.

"I hope that's a happy tear." She put both her hands on her hips.

"Yes, thank you Alice."

"Now, when I have my wedding day, you'll have to return the favor."

We both laughed and the door to my bedroom swung open as Father entered. I turned and stood up by the vanity across the room.

"Now, what if I was still getting changed, Father?!" I yelled, playfully.

"Darling Angeline…" He held his hand to his heart. "It's like your mother is here with us now."

"Father, you're going to make me cry," I said as I walked over to him.

"Now don't go doing that. We already dried her tears enough as it is," Alice remarked.

Father laughed at what she said and gently placed one hand on each side of my face. His smile, that seemed to extend from ear to ear, brightened the room all the more than it already was.

"I already knew that Calian would be the happiest man on earth today, but my…you might even make the poor guy faint upon entering!" he joked. We all laughed and headed out of the room.

"Is it already time?" I asked.

"Well, we don't exactly have many people in attendance. It's just me, Mary, Alice and Calian, of course…" Father answered.

His tribe welcomed me into their home, but they had promised never to set foot on this cursed land again. It took Calian a long time to gain their forgiveness for coming here in the first place all those years ago. They understood when he explained it was my life that was in danger. We would have another private ceremony with his family some other time. Father helped me descend the steps as Alice trailed behind, holding the end of my dress. When we got to the front door, he opened it and I could see Calian outside at the end of the path that led to the beginning of the sandbar that led to the mainland. It was high tide, and the path was no longer visible. Cal stood tall with his hands down by his sides. His hair was tied back and sun-kissed skin glimmered with the daylight. Kitchi stood beside him and a priest was in the center. I paused for a moment, then felt Father's arm intertwine with mine as he guided me down the aisle. If it weren't for him, I was sure that my legs would fold from beneath me and I'd fall straight down. My hands felt clammy and although there were barely any guests in attendance, the ones who mattered the most were all here, aside from Calian's family. White Hydrangea lined the sides of the path that we took. They went along with this day and my dress perfectly. I remember Calian finding and planting them a year or two prior. They come back every year after the dead of winter.

As I neared closer to Calian, I felt Father loosen his arm around mine and I only tightened it more. I didn't want him to leave, but at the same time knew it was necessary. He couldn't exactly get married to Calian, too… Father kissed my forehead and went off to the side, taking a seat beside Alice and Mary just a few feet away.

I looked over at the priest who held a Bible before him. He wasted no time as he began the ceremony. All I could feel were Calian's eyes on me and I couldn't help but glance over at him, my eyes glued to his as soon as we made contact. The calm that overcame me whenever I looked into them made me feel like everything was going to be okay. From what we had been through together in the past, I knew he was the one from the very start. He never failed at being by my side, even in the worst of times, and more importantly…he believed in me. When it felt like the entire world was against me, having that one person by my side that understood me both inside and out has shown me I am never truly alone. His patience and calmness through it all has brought out the best in me and some sides of me I never thought existed. Although we came from very different upbringings and traditions, it still felt like we were two pieces of the same puzzle that fit perfectly together. The priest cleared his throat, and I knew it was time for the vows. I pressed my lips together, realizing I should've likely been listening, but the entire time I was more distracted by the love of my life. Cal was first.

"I, Calian, take thee, Angeline, to be my wedded wife, to have and to hold from this day forward, for better, for worse, for richer, for poorer, in sickness and in health, to love and to cherish, till death do us part, according to God's holy ordinance; and thereto I pledge thee my faith." I couldn't believe it was finally happening. I swallowed hard and tried my best to say the same.

"I, Angeline, take thee, Calian, to be my wedded husband, to have and to hold from this day forward, for better, for worse, for richer, for poorer, in sickness and in health, to love and to cherish, till death do us part, according to God's holy ordinance; and thereto I pledge thee my faith." I could hear Father sobbing and looked over as Mary rubbed his back.

"I now pronounce you husband and wife! You may kiss the bride!" the priest announced. Before he could say the second sentence, Calian's lips were already locked on mine. The world felt like it was spinning around us and we were the only two there. I felt one of his hands as it gently touched the back of my neck, leaning me closer in until my chest was pressed up against him. As I moved back for air, I felt like a magnet to him, kissing him again and again. We turned and his fingers intertwined in mine as we lifted them up in the air as if we won the most prized gift anyone in the world could have won. More valuable than any amount of money, jewels, gold or diamonds…something that no one would ever be able to put a price on — love.

Until Death Do Us Part

28

When the ceremony was over, we all went back into the ballroom where a long table was brought in for all of us to sit at and dine. Alice had decorated the entire room in white hydrangea; even the table has several vases full of them. A musician had been hired and was playing sweet melodies from his violin. Calian walked over to my side and held out his hand.

"May I have this dance?" he asked, formally.

"Of course." I gave him my hand and followed toward the middle of the ballroom. He wrapped his arms around me as I laid my head on his shoulder and we swayed back and forth to the slow song that the violinist played.

"I have never met anyone like you," Cal said.

"Me neither, Calian."

"Although life flipped upside down when I met you, it has been a journey that I wouldn't have passed up for anything else."

"Even the tragedy that happened a few years back?" I asked, wondering his response, although I was quite sure I already knew.

"I wouldn't have rather been by anyone else's side through all that," he answered. I looked up into his eyes and brushed my lips against his. The softness in his eyes lingered, but there was now a burning desire that I felt deep in my chest. We walked back over to the table and finished eating. Calian and Father always liked to bring up their 'master plan' of a proposal that they were able to keep secret from me. They both assured one another that they would make great spies. I rolled my eyes at them and yawned, ready for bed.

"Goodnight, Father."

"Night, sweet. I'll see you in the morning." He kissed my hand, not wanting to get up from the chair he sat down in. I walked over to Alice and thanked her for all of her help, then headed upstairs beside Cal. We had both waited for this night for a very long time and it looked like it had finally come. As soon as we walked in the door of my bedroom, he quietly shut the door behind us and I pressed him up against the other side of it. His fingers rubbed across the length of my body as I was still in the dress from earlier. I turned around and felt him untie the back, as it relieved me. When the dress became loose, I shimmied out of it and this time, he pressed me against the wall, kissing my lips and then trailing down my neck, leading to my chest. The touch of his lips on my breasts sent a shiver down my spine, and I wanted to touch him in the same way. I wanted to make him shiver as I kissed every inch of his body. He began to take his shirt off and loosened his trousers until they both fell to the ground. He gently scooped me up in his arms and laid me down on the bed, sure to lie beside me as he continued kissing. When he reached below my torso, I couldn't help but put my head back in pleasure. I rolled over and straddled him on the bed, kissing his lips down to his chest.

"I want you. Now." His words came out after each gasp of air.

"Then have me." I moved my face up and pressed my lips firmly into his as I felt him push into me. I couldn't help but moan into the pillow beside his face. We made love for what seemed like hours; finishing and resting for only a bit before we started again. Eventually, we fell asleep in one another's arms.

I remember getting up to use the bathroom downstairs since that was the only one that we had and I was careful not to wake Cal. He looked so peaceful in his slumber that I wouldn't have been able to forgive myself if I ruined it for him. I shimmied back into the white dress that was still on the floor beside the bed from earlier so as not to have to open the wardrobe and cause more noise. In the bathroom, I stared into the mirror and couldn't help but see Mother in me along with Father's eyes. When I was just about to leave to head back up the stairs, I saw a fire engulfing the halls upstairs. I tried to run up the stairs, but couldn't in time to get to Father's bedroom or Calian's. The maids' room was also blocked off. As the fire traveled up the walls like a contagious disease, the roof was now billowing with smoke.

"Calian! Father!! Alice, Mary!!" I called out, choking back the smoke that I inhaled. I stumbled down the stairs and found Father.

"Come here!" He held out his arm, and I reluctantly went over to him, not wanting to leave Calian or anyone else behind. "It must have started upstairs. I fell asleep down in the ballroom. Let's go."

"But, Calian." My feet planted in the ground.

"There won't be any you or Calian if you don't come with me now," he said. I followed him out, and he dragged me all the way to the shore.

"I love you, Ange," he said, kissing my forehead upon running back inside the house.

"No!! Father!! No, No, No!" I screamed until it hurt. I fell down to my knees and watched as the house caved in from the roof, pushing the entirety of what once was my own down as easily as if it were a pile of sticks. I fell down to my knees and watched my whole world tarnish before me. The fire grew so enormous that civilians on the mainland must have seen it from afar. I heard bells ring crazily from the mainland. Help was on the way, but it wouldn't be anywhere near in time. I just continued to watch in horror. As the smoke billowed out, it seemed to gather together in the form of a man just before what used to be front steps. His appearance was completely gray from the smoke, but I could tell from his light hair and tall stature exactly who it was. He had come after all of these years to haunt me. A devilish smile spread across his face before the smoke that built him whisper off into the air, vanishing from sight.

"Please!!! Calian!! Father!!" I cried out, digging my nails into the ground. Not caring of what became of the dress any longer. Or of what became of me. I wished Father hadn't saved me because I would go on in my life, cursed. Deeply cursed. I would carry this curse with me forever. I pressed my head into the ground and wished that it would open up and I could just bury myself when I felt the presence of something familiar. As I picked my head up, I saw Kitchi. I glanced over my shoulder and saw that it was low tide. She must have come over here on her own. Animals usually ran from fire, though; let alone go toward it...

"He's gone, Kitchi. They're both gone." Saying it aloud made me cry all the more, even when I thought I had no tears left. When I put my head back down, I felt her soft head poke my back. "It's no use, they're gone." She poked me a second time and when I looked back at her, I saw that she was carefully walking to the side of the remnants of the house. I mustered up everything in me to stand up again and followed.

"Where are you going? You'll get hurt," I warned. She continued on, the brave doe that she had been named for. While we continued past the side of the house, I heard the second floor as it collapsed in on the first. My heart sank even more. Kitchi came back to me and poked me again, making sure that I was continuing to follow. She brought me all the way around toward the back of the house and rushed to where the back door had been.

"You can't go there! It's collapsing!" I screamed and ran to her side. Before my eyes were both Father and Calian lying just at the exit of the house. They were badly burned in various places, but were gasping for air and still alive. "Oh, my God! You're both alive!!" The tears rushed down my cheeks as I ran to their sides, dragging them by the arms away from the house. Calian and Father both held hands as I held the others, continuing to drag them. Alice and Mary appeared by my side and seemed to apply more strength to help them get away. Just when we were a few feet from the house, its entirety collapsed in on itself and the exit no longer remained. I heard the firemen as they reached the house and put it out.

"Help! Over here!" I called out, hoping they could hear me. After just a few minutes, they came around the house and started taking care of Father and Calian.

"You're alive, you're alive. You're both alive!" I couldn't stop screaming it repeatedly. I accompanied both of them as they were taken elsewhere and treated. Other than the burns, they were both in much better shape than anyone could have hoped.

That was the last day we stayed at the resort. After a while, they had rebuilt the building in the same place that it had been. Priest after priest came to throw holy water on it. We promised to never stay there again as the cursed land it was and the cursed land it would always continue to be.

Afterward

Lady Angeline lived a full life and kept her promise to herself and her family to never step foot on the island ever again. Although she reports feeling a pull to go back there, she never had in her lifetime — even to visit Alice and Mary. Her family later sold the island to monks who created a monastery on it in an attempt to rid it of the evil spirits that it contained.

Hundreds of years later, locals venture out to this forbidden land despite its cursed history and some never truly make it back. The visitors that stay on the mainland report that if you go late at night to look onto the path during low tide when there is a full moon, you can see a woman in a white dress as she seemingly guards the path. Some say that she is protecting people from enduring the horrors that she had to endure while there and others say that her spirit remains there in an attempt to gain vengeance on George who, even in death, attempted to murder everyone she held dear. The only one who will ever truly know is Lady Angeline herself.

Acknowledgements

Thank you to those that I have lost for always sending reminders even when you are no longer here physically. I couldn't have done this without you.

Grandma Neenee, you have always listened to me on the phone go on and on about my writing ideas. There were many times that we would laugh at silly events I'd come up with and then decide on meaningful names for characters. I miss you more than you'll ever know; let your spirit continue on.

Nonna Rose, even before I started publishing my books, you always listened to my handwritten stories that I never finished. I'm glad that I was finally able to complete them and couldn't have done it without your support!

Mom, thank you for your support in my writing and helping with book events. I'm not quite sure I could put up a canopy tent on my own that wouldn't collapse on people! Thank you for accepting payment in hugs and food!

Last, but not least thank you to my family and friends for supporting me on my writing journey and always cheering me on. I couldn't do it without you!

Charles Island Disclosure

Charles Island is located in Milford, Connecticut and is a state park. The sandbar (tombolo) between Silver Sands State Park and Charles Island over washes twice daily with tidal flooding which produces dangerous currents and undertow. No one should walk on any portion of the tombolo when it is covered with water.

Attention Hikers!

It is important to know walking all the way to Charles Island is not always possible. Low tides do not always uncover the tombolo completely. See Milford Harbor/Connecticut tide chart for tide details.

<u>NO CROSSING May 1st to September 9th due to natural area preserve for nesting birds!</u>

Turn the page for a sneak peek of another Tale of Charles Island:

The Cursed Monastery

AVAILABLE NOW

The Beginning

1

In the beginning God created the heavens and the earth. And the earth was a formless and desolate emptiness, and darkness was over the surface of the deep, and the Spirit of God was hovering over the surface of the waters. Then God said, "Let there be light"; and there was light.

(Genesis 1:1-3)

After many stormy days, the sun finally emerged from behind the clouds. The brutal heat that came was unbearable as crowds flocked to the shores to cool off. I couldn't resist the urge to follow them. Even being in the lowest level of the house was exhausting. No work could be done on the farm once the sun soared high in the sky. It would force us to wake early to get any and all work done. The farm had been in the family for a while and it was how we made a living, but things fell apart when the war came. Everything seemed to fall apart.

I felt my father's compass that he had left me clunk in my pocket as I walked into the kitchen. I treasured it most because it was the one thing that could always bring me back home, no matter how lost I was. I was somehow able to hold on to it throughout the war as, thankfully, we were not displaced, and it never left my side since. It had been a little under a year since the war ended and troops were pulled out of the thick of it. I remembered the day Father had left like it was yesterday. I thought about what he was doing out there every single second of the day. When schools closed and I had to help Mother on the farm, I would always keep an eye peeled so that I didn't miss him when he finally came home. The hope that he would someday come back never faded. I clasped my hand around the compass and felt its cold metallic case, thinking of the moments before it was even given to me.

"Lucy," he called outside when I was just thirteen years old, likely getting into trouble. I remembered I was supposed to be working and doing chores the whole time, so I thought I had been caught and would get yelled at upon my return. I made sure to saunter extra slowly, as I was in no rush to be punished.

The moment I walked closer into view of the house and the back steps, I could see the disappointment in my father's eyes, but it wasn't because of me. Several men in uniform stood behind him while Mother was on her knees, sobbing.

"Father, what is it?" I immediately asked and rushed up to him, eyeing the men in uniform.

"I need to go." He looked back at the men and they nodded as if they approved of what he had said to me.

"But where?"

"I have been summoned to war."

As soon as the last word left his mouth, Mother wailed like she had been pierced through the heart with a knife. I ran over to her and hugged her, not fully understanding at the time what this had meant for our family.

"It's okay, Mother. Father will be back. Right?" I looked over my shoulder at him and it seemed the men in uniform were rushing him in some way. He walked over to me slowly and got down to his knees, hugging Mother and me close to him. I felt Mother shaking uncontrollably and wished I could help her feel better. I had never seen her like this before.

"No matter what, we all end up together. Just remember that" he said.

When he got up and headed inside, I followed like a lost puppy dog would follow the only person who fed them. His bag had already been packed, and I immediately regretted taking so long outside and not coming in right away. It was time I would never get back with him. The men in the uniforms stood by the front door, waiting. He saluted them and asked if they could spare him a moment longer and that he would be right out. Both of them filed out, closing the door behind them. Father turned toward me and bent down so he could be more on my level and look me right in the eyes.

"Lucy, there is one lesson in life that you must know, and I am sorry you have to learn it at such a young age. There are things in life we cannot control; we must simply embrace the change and accept what is to come. While I am gone, you and your mother must look after one another.

I know you were out there avoiding your chores and that's okay. I wish you could be a child and do trouble-maker things for a bit longer, but this is the day you need to grow up and take responsibility for our family. Take care of your mother and remember, we will see each other again."

I could barely process everything he said but felt a tear stream down my cheek because he had known I was avoiding my chores all along, but he still cared for me and understood me. I pressed my head into his shoulder and let my tears pour out, soaking his shirt.

"Lucy." He pushed me away from him and pulled out a handkerchief, wiping my tears. "Hold out your hand."

I obeyed.

He placed something in my hand that was far too big for me to hold and gave me a shock as soon as it touched my skin. When he moved his hand away from it, I saw a compass that had four inscriptions on it: north, south, east and west in cursive. The arrow pointed in between the North and East signs.

"You see this?" He pointed to where the arrow was, and I nodded my head. "This will make sure you are never lost. Do not ever part from it."

"Won't you need it?" I asked.

"Not where I'm going. And in any case, they will likely give us one if we do need direction. I want you to keep this on you so you never lose your way." He closed my fingers over the compass and wrapped his arm around me, hugging me one final time. He kissed me on the forehead and opened the door to leave.

I wanted to beg him to stay or hide him somewhere, so the men in uniform didn't have to take him away. Instead, I ran over to the window to watch as Father walked to the truck with his duffel bag over his shoulder. Mother ran from around back and he stopped and turned, opening up his arms wide to catch her. She practically threw herself onto him and he spun her around; her feet were fully off the ground. They kissed and hugged for so long that I barely noticed my breath fogging up the window that I pressed my face against, yearning to be out there too.

I picked my hand up and looked at the compass again, holding it close to my chest as if hugging it was like hugging Father. It was nowhere close, but it was something.

That day had been at least ten years ago, and I still clung to the compass just as I had when I was just a young girl. Having a reminder of who I was even when I had thought I lost myself completely kept me grounded. Something in me told me to use it that day and go wherever it took me. I wasn't exactly sure how, but I was desperate for answers.

About the Author

Marissa is the author of a memoir and the Tales of Charles Island series. Marissa mostly writes fictional stories and began by journaling and writing screenplays in elementary school. She spends much of her time with her pets aside from traveling to new places and teaching. Born and raised in Connecticut, she holds New England close to her heart and many of her stories are based in the suburbs of New England.

She has a deep and profound respect for people with special needs as her first job in her field was a special educator. Marissa found her voice through writing. While in high school, she was the editor of the Arts and Entertainment section of the school newspaper. She pursued a degree in Education, minoring in English literature and Anthropology. Later, she went back to school to better understand Autism and graduated with a Master's in Special Education.

Marissa would love to hear from you. Use the links below to connect & hear about upcoming books:

Visit Marissa's Website:

www.mystywrites.com

Instagram:

www.instagram.com/_mysty_writes/

Amazon Page:

www.amazon.com/author/marissadangelo